"This is not a thriller, but a brilliantly constructed piece of existentialism that addresses fundamental issues within a distinctly modern American context. Five years after a murder, Topp is still utterly at a loss about how or why he should carry on living, and engaged in friendships which he finds essential but unfulfilling. Yet the themes covered are not simply universal but also reflective of the specific issues which dominate modern America. Many of the characters are struggling financially, hovering on the edge economically, dependent on others and fearful of what awaits them. Yet it is the topic of guns which contemporary readers will find most powerful. Topp's wife has been killed in the most horrifying way, but Peterson never lectures us or presents a factual debate about gun death. Art's only form of recreation with his closest male friend is to go to the shooting range, and we are given a beautiful description of a hunter bagging a full-grown caribou. We are brought to the point where we understand the appeal of guns, and it is the sense of power they give combined with the terrible ease with which they are acquired which does most to teach us how terrible this blight is."

- Stephen Grant, author of *Spanish Light*

ADVANCE PRAISE FOR
GUNMETAL BLUE

"Joseph G. Peterson doesn't write books—he builds literary houses out of brick-solid sentences and fills those houses with characters who understand the effort it takes to survive. Narrated by Art Topp, a widower, a hapless father, and the city's laziest private eye, this is a story of family and guns and murder, and the compassion it takes to overcome all three. Here, women who should be retired still wait tables. Here, daughters can't stand their dads. Here, a best friend shoots off an Uzi to feel alive but still lives at home with his ancient mom. A bitter husband shows up for coffee with a loaded Glock. A dead wife speaks advice from the other side. I've read and greatly enjoyed all of Joseph Peterson's books but *Gunmetal Blue* is sadder and funnier and more tender than anything he's written. Chicago, lock up your guns and open your bookshelves to let Joe Peterson in. *Gunmetal Blue* is a book that wants every life to matter. Read these pages and you'll understand why."

- Dave Newman, author of *The Poem Factory* and *Two Small Birds*

T0143862

GUN METAL BLUE

OTHER BOOKS BY JOSEPH G. PETERSON

Novels

Short Stories

GUNMETAL BLUE

JOSEPH G. PETERSON

TORTOISE BOOKS

CHICAGO, IL

For my brothers, Mike & Bob

Did you kiss the dead body

Harold Pinter

Police Seek Clues in Jewelers Row Killing
By Martin Dorsey

A 42-year-old woman was found dead of multiple gunshot wounds Tuesday evening in a building in the 200 block of South Wabash Avenue. Police spokesperson Lt. Marc Céspedes says the woman, Adeleine Topp, was discovered shortly after 6:00 p.m. in the offices of the Triple A Detective AAAgency by her husband Art Topp, the agency's owner. Chicago police are investigating whether the murder was related to Topp's work as a private detective, but stress that they haven't ruled out any suspects. Funeral services will be held 10:00 a.m. Tuesday at Drake & Sons Funeral Home, followed by internment at Rosehill Cemetery.

PART I: SHOT

I tip the cabdriver and head up the hill to the cemetery. It was such a day five years ago, cloudless and coldish, that we buried my wife, and now revisiting this cemetery puts me in mind of that day.

What parts of that time do I want to forget? What parts do I want to remember?

I sincerely want to forget telling my daughter her mother had just been killed.

I sincerely want to forget the look on my daughter's face when I told her her mother had just been killed.

I sincerely want to forget the sound of her book bag dropping in the hallway as I told her her mother had just been killed.

The sound of her book bag—*clunk*—and then: What do you mean, Dad?

Your mother was shot and killed at my office.

What?

Your mother's body was found at my office. She was shot and killed.

Dad, Mom never visits your office. You've got to be joking.

Shot her not once but seventeen times.

Daddy.

I wish I were joking.

Daddy, where's Mom? Please.

They took her away to the morgue.

I want to forget that my daughter had to live through that.

I want to forget that my daughter had to watch her mother buried.

I want to forget that I stood with my high school daughter over her mother's grave.

I want to forget that it was a day such as this that destroyed my family life.

I had a wonderful family life. We had a wonderful family life. We live to have family, to build a family, to live a life within the family. We don't live to watch the family destruct. But apparently so. Apparently we were put on earth to learn both happy truths and terrible truths. I can't bear the terrible truths. I can't bear them.

Now you're feeling sorry for yourself.

And so I am.

The leaves on the trees are falling. They wiggle on the stem and the wind pulls them away.

The eternal hearse pulls into an eternal graveyard trailing terrible truths, which are eternal. Who is it today that has come to die?

You're just depressed.

Am not.

Yes you are.

A line of vehicles pulls into the cemetery. A freshly dug grave is open, right next to my wife's. I walk up behind to see who has died this time. Family members, grief-stricken, stumble out of three limos. An assortment of other folks step from their cars. And behind those, a school bus, from which a bunch of high school kids tumble. Young high school girls are crying just like my Meg cried on the day her mom was buried. Boys wearing football jerseys weep openly. Confused.

Catch them, Meg told me after the funeral.

Catch who?

Daddy, this is no time for joking. Whatever you do, promise me you'll catch whoever did this.

I didn't know we raised such an uncompromising person.

Get who killed Mom. Please.

I don't know if I can do this, darling. Honestly, I'm too close to the case. I don't know if I can catch who did this. It's too ghoulish. I'm suffocating, if you know what I mean.

I'm suffocating. It's me who's dying here. It's your daughter. Find out who killed Mom. I don't trust anyone else to get it right. You must find out who did it.

But the cops are already on the case, and until it's solved, I'm one of the subjects of their investigation.

You are?

Well they said in the paper they haven't ruled anyone out. I don't want to mess it up. Conflict of interest, that sort of thing. Honey, please. Let the police work it out. I have absolute faith in them.

Still, Daddy. You must find out who did this. I won't take no for an answer.

No.

Daddy!

OK, I'll see what I can do.

Please.

OK, but no guarantees.

And another thing, I hate you so much for taking Mom away from me I promise I will never talk to you again, ever!

•

It was in this cemetery, too—Ha! Ha!—I met Rita, all those years ago.

She was mourning the death of her mom—crying near her mom's gave, which just so happens was near my wife's grave.

From the ashes grows a flower, or so I thought.

You're rhyming again.

Blurt. Blurt.

Pop. Pop. Pop.

•

Rita's mom had died in a car accident.

I didn't dare tell her how my wife died. I only told her she'd died in an accident, too. Rita assumed from this that I meant car accident and I have never corrected her.

How did your mom die? I asked her. She had showed up to the cemetery carrying fresh-cut flowers.

Car accident.

She wore a veil, which put her in a different era even though she was at least ten years younger than me.

Pretty veil.

I didn't know what else to wear. I'm in mourning.

How did it happen?

My mom's car was hit by a bus while she was waiting for the light to turn. I was at work when they called me to tell me. How did your wife die?

Accident.

See, she said. The road is a dangerous place. My mother's death has taught me this.

Yes.

When did she die?

Three months ago.

Same with my wife.

My condolences.

Same same.

How are you getting on?

I miss her. I do. She was all I had. Now I feel orphaned. How about you?

Numb.

We stood over our respective graves. Each paying silent respect. I pulled a few weeds that had sprouted up near my wife's tombstone. Then the two of us found a bench, sat down, and talked.

Where you from?

West Loop. How about you?

Same, as a matter of fact.

What do you do?

An assortment of things. How about you?

I wait tables. Hardest thing though, to wait on people. I have the hardest time serving people now that my mother's gone.

Yeah, I know what you mean.

You do?

Sure.

Because I break down two or three times a day crying, for what I don't know. I didn't think it was going to be so difficult getting over my mom.

What's your name?

Rita.

Hi Rita, I'm Art.

Hey.

Hey.

Some day, huh.

You'd think it spring, only the leaves have just fallen off the trees.

Does it bode a mild winter?

Are winters ever mild in Chicago?

I suppose not.

If every day were like this, I could take it. It's the cold that gets me. This is sweater weather.

That's a nice one you have on, Rita.

Thanks. My mom has knitted every sweater I own.

The one you have on is very lovely.

Thank you. I'm making a vow with you.

With me?

I vow to only wear sweaters my mom has made. That's my vow. Oh, and another thing. I vow to do nothing in excess.

She smiled at me.

I suppose it depends what your limits are, I said.

I suppose you would be right.

Perhaps sitting near her that day—three months after my wife passed—made me feel less alone. I don't know. Perhaps it was the fact that she had suffered some loss of her own which made me feel as if she might understand me. Understand what I was going through. Or perhaps it was that lovely sweater. But after a bit, I asked her if she wanted to get some lunch with me.

How 'bout getting a bite to eat, Rita?

I hope you're not picking me up.

Certainly not. Why, are you available?

My mom just died. I want you to know that before I agree to go to lunch with you.

I'm only offering lunch.

All right then, let's go.

•

It was the meal after the funeral—the meal to conquer grief—that I most looked forward to on that terrible day we buried my wife.

This is the one thing I want to remember. The meal after I buried my wife.

I had been ravenously hungry, though I don't remember being hungry. It wasn't until I had started to eat that I realized just how hungry I was. I was ravenous. Gluttonous. I felt like a vampire feasting on the blood of a thousand virgins.

When I couldn't eat any more, I continued to eat. I ate myself into a catatonic torpor and passed out in the corner while the other mourners around me caught up with each other. I was surrounded by the funeral crowd: the part of the family that only gets together at funerals. They were catching up on each other's lives since the last funeral. I couldn't take it. I thought I would scream. Instead, I sat somberly in the corner eating my meal. My nose down at my plate trying to consume myself into oblivion.

•

Go ahead, honey. Have seconds.

Those were Adeleine's words. That was her mantra: Have seconds, eat more. Adeleine was hugely appetitive. She loved to cook. She wasn't one of those who was afraid of food. She ate. What's more, she loved to watch me eat.

How about seconds, Art?

My weight.

I don't care about your weight; I married you for your appetite. It's your appetite I'm here to serve.

Those were Adeleine's words. It's your appetite I'm here to serve.

Without Adeleine, how was I ever going to eat again?

She was that rare cook who cooked equally well from a cookbook or from her own imagination. I loved everything she made.

What's for dinner tonight? I would say, coming home from work.

Beef Stroganoff in a vodka cream sauce, Caesar salad with anchovies, cold borscht, mushroom barley soup, pickled herring, sardines, liverwurst, stuffed green peppers, fat pickles and rye bread and chocolate cake with cookies. I've two bottles of wine open and that bottle of chilled vodka to wash it down.

Her Beef Stroganoff—to die for—was from an ancient family recipe. Her grandmother brought it back from Leningrad, Russia. She never passed her cooking down to our daughter, Meg. Meg is a stick. She has never liked eating. She was always fussy; she never showed an interest. As a result, the recipe for the Beef Stroganoff went with Adeleine to the grave, and I haven't had the likes of it since. I don't expect to.

•

Rita and I went to a quiet Sicilian restaurant, Giovanna's, just down the road a block or two from the cemetery. We ordered family style: bread, sausage, hand-rolled rotini in a mushroom sauce with speck, gnocchi, veal cutlets sautéed in wine sauce, braised chicken in a lemon sauce with capers, a cheese plate, marinated peppers and a bottle of Chianti.

We talked about this and that.

What's your zodiac?

You're not trying to pick me up?

PETERSON

No. Why would I do that?

I don't know. My mom just died.

How about some more gnocchi?

Yes. I love gnocchi.

The gnocchi here is good.

It is better at Leo's down the street.

Yes, their gnocchi is very good.

I like the pesto better here.

The Chianti's good.

Here, have more.

Thank you.

Bread.

Sure.

Butter.

Yeah.

Olive oil.

Please.

More wine.

Pour it on.

I filled her glass.

To the dead.

Here here, she said approvingly. May they rest in peace. She promptly made the sign of the cross and I looked on solemnly.

The waiter stopped by.

Thanks for coming. I was dying of thirst.

Can I get you anything?

Another bottle of wine.

More bread.

I'm famished.

Me too.

Something about grief makes me eat.

What do you do, Art?

All sorts of things. What about you?

I wait tables. I work part-time at a nail salon.

I like your nails.

I did them myself.

I raised my glass again. Here's to the living.

The living, she said.

Clink, clink.

The afternoon light began to wane and we were laughing over something or another and then apropos nothing at all, she said:

Where do you want to go now?

Let's go downtown. My office is across the street from a lovely hotel.

Lets, she said. Why not.

And so our relationship was born.

•

I pull up behind the students who have gathered at the graveside of the world's latest victim.

Who died? I ask someone—a pimple-faced student standing next to me. He's wearing a pink housecoat and slippers.

A guy named Albert Volares. A football player. He died in a head-on-head tackle.

How old?

Fifteen.

Jesus.

I didn't know him.

Oh?

I'm just here to get out of school.

The priest stands reading psalms. Valley of evil, etc.

The mother weeps uncontrollably. The father holds her with both arms and tries to comfort her. Apparently it was her only child.

We wait to die. Why else were we put on this earth but to learn truths? Terrible truths.

Are you talking to me? the kid asks.

I suppose I am talking.

Did you know him?

Who?

Albert.

No.

Then why are you here?

Same reason as you. To get out of school.

The boy looks at me like I'm crazy.

The priest says something about the dead boy and then a picture of the boy with a little biography of the boy is circulated through the crowd.

ALBERT VOLARES

He is survived by

His parents
Albert and Mona Volares
He loved Pokémon, Battlefield, Minecraft, pizza and football.
He wanted to be an FBI agent.
He was loved by everyone who knew him.
He will be missed.
He was a person full of promise.

The picture is of an astonishingly handsome young man with the cheekbones and hooked nose of an Aztec warrior.

A line forms behind a pile of dirt and one by one people grab the shovel, a silver spade, and toss a clod of dirt on his casket.

•

This is one thing I want to remember from the week my wife died: I want to remember the pile of dirt that we all stood behind. I want to remember that I had stood near that pile of dirt with the spade in my hand. I want to remember that I had shoveled the dirt without cease upon her tomb until she was completely buried. I want to remember the weight of the earth in my hands as I threw it down upon my beloved wife's grave. I want to remember the feeling of labor, the feeling of using my arms and legs to lift the earth and hurl it upon the box of her coffin. I bought her the most expensive coffin money could buy, and that day, tossing dirt against her coffin, I realized it was utterly the wrong decision to make. I should have buried her in a plain pine box. I should have sent her to earth the humblest way imaginable, and yet the coffin gleamed back at me as I hurled dirt upon it, to remind me how much I paid for it. I remember lifting the dirt and praying in my heart of hearts to be humble. I don't know who I prayed to, but I believe I was talking to the truest purest aspect of me. Be humble, I exhorted myself as I flung dirt upon her grave. Be humble, thou who hurlest the dirt upon thine wife. Be humbler than the dirt.

The undertaker and a couple of Adeleine's uncles tried to slow me down. They tried to politely remove the shovel from my hands, but I wasn't going to let them. I pushed them away. Step aside. This was between me and my wife. Be humble, ye who buriest thine wife, and do what labor she will ask of you. Do it without complaint. And so it was. I threw the dirt as if I were fulfilling a sacred obligation. I threw all the dirt, not just a spadeful. The sweat fell down my brow and into the dirt and my massive chest heaved and when I was done I set the spade in the earth and removed a handkerchief and as I looked up at the great oak tree under which she was buried I saw a gathering of crows and I knew that what I had done was the most righteous thing I have ever accomplished.

Then I looked over at my daughter Meg. She had a stunned look on her face. She looked at me as if she couldn't believe what had just happened. She watched her dad bury her mother with a fury that suggested he had been waiting for this moment for years. She watched her dad dispatch her own mother, and when I walked over to her to explain, she turned away from me.

What the hell were you doing, Dad?

I was trying to do right by your mom.

You looked like you couldn't get her in the earth fast enough.

That's not it at all.

Well how do you explain it? You were like a madman over there.

My mother-in-law came up to me. I reached over to give her a comforting hug and she slapped me, then walked away. Adeleine's father walked up behind her and told me confidentially that my behavior was the most appalling thing he had seen in his life, and he had seen some appalling behavior in his day.

Meg shunned me the rest of the day.

At the meal after the funeral, my daughter played hostess. But people had been turned off by my digging. Meg was so angry with me she shunned me when I went over to her to try to explain yet again. Our relationship has never quite recovered.

It was at this time the food was brought out: ribs, pork chops, fried chicken, piles of the stuff. The place smelled like a barbecue pit. I grabbed a bib and found a table in the corner. Friends and family members came to offer their condolences. I flagged them away and ate more food than I had ever eaten in my life: three slabs of ribs, eight or nine pieces of chicken, countless hot links, slaw, cornbread, and the haunches of a spit-rotated hog. I ate until I passed out. The next day I shit forever and cried.

•

I stand at Albert Volares' grave while family members shovel dirt onto his casket. I was raised Catholic, and have retained some vestigial sense of intimate prayer, though I no longer pray. Instead, I just close my eyes.

We live to die.

Now you're just feeling sorry for yourself.

I suppose I am.

I suppose you are.

•

Daddy, find out who did this.

I don't know if I can.

Please.

It's too much for me. I'm suffocating, if you know what I mean.

It's me. I'm the one who's suffocating over here. You must.

Honey.

You must.

Please.

I won't forgive you if you don't. And another thing, I hate you so much for taking Mom away from me I promise I will never talk to you again, ever!

The truth is, I didn't have the heart to track down my wife's murderer. I didn't want to find out. In truth, I was afraid to find out. I expected that the person who killed Adeleine had been activated by one of my jobs. I couldn't bring myself to verify this had been the case. If I discovered that the man who had killed Adeleine was activated by one of my jobs, it would be more than I could deal with. Worse, it would destroy Meg.

⊙

Before all this, years before, I had lost a job in telecom. I was searching for ways to regain a foothold in the economy when I came up with the idea to open my own shop as a detective.

I told Adeleine about my idea and waited to see what she said.

Why do you want to be a private eye? she asked.

Why not, Adeleine?

Because there are so many other wonderful things to do with your life.

She was right, but I wasn't going to let her be right on this point, especially since it was me who had been washed out of the economy and who was searching for relevance. So I told her: I like this detective life.

You like the 'idea' of this life, but what do you know about it? Is your heart really set on becoming a private eye?

What does that mean?

It means, do you really want to be a private eye, or do you want to do it because of books you've read on the subject?

I've never really read any books on the subject.

Then where did you get the idea?

I don't know. Though I did like James Garner in *The Rockford Files*.

But that was a TV show. It's not what the job is really like.

I don't know what the job is really like, but I imagine it's like any other job.

How so?

It is what you make of it.

It's long boring hours doing lots of boring things for little to no pay.

Honey, I objected. It's what I want to do. We don't need to analyze it, do we?

Well I want you to think it over, make sure you're happy.

I am happy, I said. I have you.

That's not going to be enough to sustain you.

It'll be enough to sustain me.

•

Later, when I started obsessively shooting at the range with Cal, she raised the issue again.

Is the reason why you want to be a private detective because you like guns?

And to be honest, she had a point. I had to acknowledge that.

I suppose that could be part of it.

But don't you see? Shooting guns at a shooting range with your buddy is a lot different from actually shooting someone. If you get a license to carry that thing, don't you realize you may have to use it?

Yeah, of course.

You're not bothered by this?

Why should I be bothered by this?

Because by carrying a gun you may either have to use it or...

Or what?

Or someone may use their gun on you!

It's a dangerous business.

Yes. But are you willing to take on the risk of such a business?

Why not? What more do I have to do with my life?

You can do anything under the sun.

Like what?

Like, you could do something important.

I wasn't made for important things.

Not important important. Just something useful, like teaching...

I already told you. I don't read books.

Think it over. Think over what you're doing. If after thinking it over, taking into consideration all of the risks, you still want to do it, then I support you one hundred and ten percent. But remember the monstrosity you evoke may come home to haunt you.

I don't know why she said that, but she did say it, and I never forgot it.

•

After a few days I came to her. She was in the kitchen cooking one of her Beef Stroganoff meals. An open bottle of Merlot was on the counter.

Well, I have something to tell you.

She looked at me, her eyes bright with expectation.

I'm going through with it.

I wiped my mouth and tamped the sweat on my brow, and Adeleine didn't say anything, so I went on.

I found an office downtown on Wabash Avenue and I've located a secretary, Wanda Jones. She's Welsh.

Adeleine looked a little crestfallen, as if she were hoping I was going to tell her something else. Like: Honey, I've made a decision...Yes?...I've decided to be a high school teacher...You have? Oh, wonderful! I knew you would do the right thing! Instead I'd told her what she'd least wanted to hear. And I was committed, so I had to keep going.

I found an office in a building on South Wabash Avenue. And a secretary. She's Welsh. I'm having a shingle made and I start work on Monday. I'm going to be a detective.

Yes.

Yes. I'm calling my business Triple A Detective AAAgency.

She looked crestfallen, as if she had suddenly realized she'd married the wrong man.

It's not what it's cracked up to be. Believe me. But if it's what you want to do...fine.

Thanks, honey.

I went to embrace her, and instead of reaching her arms around me, she held them by her side.

•

Now I sit in my office all day waiting for the phone to ring.

I sit so long in my office waiting for the phone to ring I wonder who it is I am.

When the phone does ring I pick it up and answer it.

Good afternoon, I say, as friendly as can be. This is Triple A.

Triple who? the voice says, trailing off.

Triple A Detective AAAgency.

Oh. I must have the wrong number.

Oh.

I sit in my office all day and the calls I get are all wrong numbers if I get any calls.

I wait in my office waiting for a call. When none arrive, I knock off for the day.

Wanda...

Yes, Art.

I'm knocking off for the day.

Yes.

Would you be so kind to close up before you leave?

Of course, Art. No problem.

•

I call Cal and we drive out to the gun range.

Cal shoots a well-oiled and carefully tended full-auto vintage Uzi 9mm carbine with the extending metal stock that he was blessed enough to inherit from his uncle Benny Calabrese who himself had mob connections going all the way back to the island of Sicily and who also died of old age, though why he needed an Uzi, not to mention what he might have used it for, Cal can't say. Lucky, though, for Cal, when his uncle kicked off he got the gun. He had to go through all the FFL rigamarole to start taking it to the range, but he got it for free, so he's lucky. He shoots it like he knows it too: knows how lucky he is.

I prefer something a bit more delicate. I like the original Ruger Standard model .22 caliber with suppressor. I picked mine up at a pawnshop for under a hundred bucks. It's pitted with a bit of rust, but I like the gun. I call his a blurt gun. He calls mine a pussy gun. Compared to his, I suppose it is, but it's a fun gun to go plinking with. Most people shoot better with a smaller gun.

That's a pussy gun, he says poppy-cocking around me.

So what? I like it.

Fine by me, Art, if you want to stick with it, but it would be so much better if you actually hit the target.

I do my best. But it ain't easy with you leering over my shoulder.

I'm not leering. I'm just watching what an idiot does with a pussy gun.

We go shooting back and forth, slapping each other on the back between turns. He shreds the target. I take aim and miss. Reload, miss. It's all part of our routine. He wears plugs, I wear muffs to cut down damage to our ears and shout above the noise. We both wear safety glasses. And I am shooting a .22, so I don't get the same recoil. Only the smell is full. That gunpowder smell.

Cal steps into the lane. Sets his ammo down. He keeps cursing about this girl.

Shoot her right there in the cunt, he shouts, taking aim, and off goes the gun. *BLURT. BLURT. RAT TAT TAT TAT TAT.* Cartridge brass bouncing all over the place.

Got her right there! he says, very smugly.

That's not very nice, I say. Under the conditions...

Under what conditions, Art? She wasn't a very nice girl.

But Cal you're forgetting something...

What, that it's only a paper target?

No. You just can't pretend the target is a woman. It's not fair.

Why's not?

Because under the conditions...she can't shoot back.

And if she did shoot back, she'd probably miss.

Maybe, maybe not, Cal. Or maybe she'd shoot your nuts off just for being a jackass.

Hmm. Maybe so.

He steps back. We reset the target and I step into the lane. I take aim with my Ruger and go *Pop. Pop. Pop.*

Did I tell you I had a date last night, Art?

You're hung over, I tell him, stepping aside.

He steps into the lane and picks up the Uzi: *Blurt. Blurt. Blurt.*

The bitch, he says, shooting at the target again as if it were a woman.

How'd it go?

Lousy. *RAT TAT TAT TAT.* I met her at the track. Should know better than to meet a woman at the track. *RAT TAT TAT TAT.* We left after the fifth race. She wanted me to go shopping with her. So I took her to the mall. We must have walked around that mall for three hours holding hands. At one point in an elevator we started kissing. I bought her a pair of shoes and some perfume. And then...

He goes into target shredding mode. Blasting away. When he's through, he sets it down and steps back and I step into the lane. *Pop. Pop. Pop.*

So tell me about her, Cal, I say, trying to figure out what's wrong with the sighting of my gun because I don't seem able to hit the target like I want. The sights on this one don't adjust. Rust. So it must be me or the gun. I can't decide.

I met her at the track, Cal says. Should know better than meet a woman at the track. We left after the fifth race. She wanted me to go shopping with her. So I took her to the mall. We must have walked around that mall three hours holding hands. At one point in an elevator we started kissing. I bought her a pair of shoes and some perfume. And then...

You told me all that already.

So I did.

So you did.

I step back and he steps into the lane. He puts up a new target and goes to town: *Blurt. Blurt. Blurt.*

And then I thought we were headed to my car in the parking lot, Cal says, but she flagged a cab! Wait, where are you going, I said. *Blurt. Blurt. Blurt.* Home, she said. I'll take you home, I said. No need, she said, I'll take a cab. But wait, I said. And no sooner did I say that then she was off. Gone with the wind. I must have spent two fifty on her.

He pauses from his shooting and looks at me until I get the full implication of what he's saying.

Two hundred and fifty dollars?

Yes. Two-fifty. He goes back to shooting. *RAT TAT TAT TAT TAT.*

Did you even get her name? I yell above the noise of his gun.

Maria or something…a pretty little Mexican. It gave me a lift holding her like that in the elevator. For a moment I thought things in my life were about to change. When I told her I was still living with my mom, I think I noticed disappointment.

Did you tell her your mom is flexible?

He pauses from his shooting to consider my question, and then he goes back to shooting. *Blurt. Blurt. Blurt.* When he's done, he steps back, and I step into the lane. *Pop. Pop. Pop.*

She said she doesn't believe in guys who live with their moms.

What does that mean?

What do you mean, what does that mean? It means she flagged the first cab she could find and disappeared.

But not until after you spent two-fifty on her.

Yes. Not until then.

I continue shooting trying not to be distracted by Cal, but I'm plenty distracted, so my shooting is all over the place. *Pop. Pop. Pop.*

You suck, Art.

I do my best with your palavaring. I find it distracting. *Pop. Pop. Pop.*

When I met her I felt lucky all of a sudden, Art. You have no idea. As if my luck were changing in an instant. You gotta understand. I've never been lucky.

Yes. I know.

So to meet this girl and be off with her . . . it made me feel lucky.

I understand.

He loads up his Uzi while I shoot and when he's done he asks: Do you want me to load a clip up for you?

Sure, go ahead.

Pop. Pop. Pop.

Like I was saying. I was on top of the world. I wouldn't have spent all that money on her if I knew how it was going to end. Believe me, I'm not a fool. I like to think I'm a better judge of human character than that. She didn't seem the type to screw me for two-fifty.

You say you screwed her?

I step back to make way for him. He motors the target back down to us, changes it, motors it back out. Then he pulls a 9mm Luger from out of nowhere.

See, if you only aim, Art, like I aim, and watch your breathing, and keep your hand steady, you might actually hit the target. But I'm watching you and your hands are jerking all over the place and there ain't even any power in that pussy gun to make your hand shake.

I like that Luger.

It's what got me fired from the railroad.

Oh yeah. How so?

When I was working at the Union Pacific as a brakeman I got canned for 'reckless behavior.'

How do you get fired for reckless behavior?

You only get fired for reckless behavior when someone higher up don't like you. If they have no other reason to fire you then they choose 'reckless behavior.'

But what about the union? Didn't they protect you?

Well to tell the truth, Art, I'd been caught shooting at coyotes in the railroad yard with this Luger. I'd shoot them and skin them out and sell the pelts. And one of the supervisors was watching me through his binoculars and caught me shooting. That's when I got fired for reckless behavior. Then my dad passed, and not long after he died I started receiving checks from his insurance policy.

He takes aim until he empties all the rounds in his Luger. Then he puts it down and picks up the Uzi and starts shooting single-shot.

About this girl I met at the track...I got close to fucking her in the elevator. I thought I was going to get lucky for sure, so I told her we could go back to my place. She would have done it in the elevator, too. When I told her about my mom, though, something inside of her broke.

It's OK, pally, I tell him. It's OK. It happens.

It makes me feel like shit when it happens to me. *RAT. TAT. TAT. TAT.*

Well she'll come to no good.

Of course she won't. *RAT. TAT. TAT. TAT.* She'll find someone else to do it to. That's the way with women like these.

He clears out and I step into the lane and he gives me space to shoot until I empty the clip. He hands me more loaded clips as I need them. I shoot mostly in silence, and for once I start hitting the target.

Maybe it's you, I tell Cal.

Maybe me? How so, Art?

If you just shut up for a minute and let me shoot rather than talk to me and distract me, I can actually hit the target.

Ha—Art! You just hit the target because for once you got lucky, unlike me with that girl.

I suppose I am lucky. *Blurt. Blurt. Blurt.*

You are lucky, Art. You have no idea, he says, stepping up to the line for one more round going *Blurt Blurt Blurt* with the shells flying all over the place, and when he's through he pulls his safety glasses off his face and smiles at me as if he were the Red Baron just finished blasting away at some poor fool staring at the sun.

Feels good, don't it? He smiles at me.

Yessir. It does. It always feels good. Whenever I'm feeling blue, it's nice to shoot.

Yessir, it is.

•

Hey, wait a second. You're rhyming again.

I suppose I am.

Blurt. Blurt.

Pop. Pop. Pop.

•

After shooting, I visit Rita.

Rita works the counter. She smokes more than she should smoke. Smiles less than she should smile and complains her tips are bad. Her joints ache. Her teeth hurt. Besides that, she's a bundle of joy.

When I visit her these days I feel like a dog sniffing over a dead corpse.

As opposed to a living corpse?

Our relationship is a corpse.

Whether it's a living corpse or a dead corpse remains to be seen.

I walk through the doors of the restaurant and try to smile at Rita. I try to imitate the smile I used to smile at her when we were first in love.

When were we in love?

Were we ever in love?

Love.

I smile an approximate smile at Rita, not a real smile. My smile when I walk through the doors is just like our relationship. Our relationship is an approximate relationship, not a real relationship.

I should have never become a waitress, she says when I sit down at the counter.

What would you rather do?

She hands me a cup of coffee.

Anything under the sun.

Like what?

Like what I just said, anything under the sun. I'd get out of Chicago and move south. Head to Florida or something. Become a bartender at one of those beach resorts. That's what I'd like to do. But working in Chicago. For one I can't stand the cold, and with another winter coming on I feel like a fool being stuck here waiting for it. No way out.

But Chicago has things Florida doesn't have.

Like what?

Spring and fall.

She laughs. Ha. Ha. It's cold here most of the year, and when it's not cold it's hot.

Is not.

Is too.

Is not.

You only say is not because you've got a faulty memory.

Yes. Now I'll agree with you there. It's a faulty memory that keeps me plugging away.

It's a faulty memory that's going to land you in an institution sooner than you think. Alzheimer's disease.

There's perks though, I point out. For one: I keep forgetting I hate my work, and that allows me to keep going to it in the morning.

It's probably what keeps you loving me too, by that logic. You keep loving me because you're always forgetting that you hate me.

Not true. Not true.

Your problem is, Art...

Wait a second—I have a problem?

Your problem is...Let me finish here...your problem is, you're faithful like a dog.

I didn't know fidelity was a problem.

It can be a problem. Too much fidelity can definitely be a problem.

So can infidelity.

You're too faithful to your wife's memory.

It's who I am.

Well.

Well.

Well?

I can't forget her...

Nobody's asking you to forget. I haven't forgotten my mom. All's we're asking here is you learn to let it go.

Let what go?

Let the grief go.

It is gone. Poof.

It is?

It's the fifth anniversary of her burial, that's all.

It's the fifth anniversary of mom's, and look at me. I'm still standing. You look like you were just hit by a truck. You're suffering too much. Put it behind you, Art.

Gee, aren't you friendly today?

It's just this job...

Rita sets a platter of eggs and bacon in front of me, refreshes my coffee, and gives me a small orange juice that she pulled from a dispenser.

And I'm tired. She attempts a smile. I never can figure out why they settled in Chicago.

Why who?

The original people who settled Chicago. Such a godawful place. Too cold or too hot.

Honey, what are you complaining about the cold for? It's a beautiful day out there.

I felt winter out there today. And I don't like winter. My joints permanently ache from the cold.

Then why don't you move to Florida? Or some spa town with hot springs, Epson salt, and mud?

Epsom salt. Easy for you to say, Art. With all your millions...You can go down to Fort Lauderdale at the drop of a hat and snap up one of those mansions in...what do they call it? I saw a show on it the other day. Little Venice. Yeah. You with your millions! Solving crime. I'm trying not to laugh. Some of us, however, have to work for a living. Some of us actually have to do something to earn a living.

But Rita...Look, you don't like the heat, either. You're always complaining about the heat. It's either too hot or too cold for you.

I like the heat, Art. Don't get me wrong. It's just this heat—this stupid, muggy Chicago heat—I don't like it. Never have.

She frowns at me and sighs.

Chicago has an unrepenting heat. Just like it has an unrepenting cold. And I just don't like it.

What's unrepenting?

You know what I mean...

Are you talking about the Catholic Church? Unrepenting? Maybe you ought to see a priest.

And confess my sins?

You don't have any sins.

Working in this dump is a sin. Staying with you for five years is probably a sin too.

Nothing in the Old Testament says staying with a guy like me is a sin.

Oh, it's a sin, Art. Believe you me. This funny relationship we have is a sin. The way you smile at me these days. I feel it in my bones. It's a sin.

Are you confessing something to me? Spill it out. I'm here to listen.

You know what I'm saying.

I do?

Let this be a warning to you, Art. My love only goes so deep.

What does that mean?

You know what it means.

And then I'll be out on my ear living with my mom?

Just like all your other loser friends.

Speaking of Cal, he and his mom live off his father's life-insurance policy. That was his big reveal today.

That's nice. I suppose he plans on gambling it all away.

He doesn't want to, but he can't help himself.

He should get a job instead of mooching off his parents.

I think he's tried. He had a job at Waste Management all lined up but he forgot to go to the interview.

Well then, he's crazy. Tell him to see a shrink.

He'd never see a shrink. Are you kidding me!

No, I don't suppose he would. Art, you sure know how to pick 'em!

I eat my eggs and bacon and watch Rita work the line. She looks tired, exhausted. She looks like someone who left this place years ago, her eyes have left this place, but her body is still here. Her body is trying to figure out how to get to that place her eyes already escaped to. Her eyes went somewhere— south, perhaps—but she remains here waiting and waiting for something—for me perhaps, for her chances to up turn, for an opportune moment to quietly slip away when no one is looking. In the meantime she goes about her work and complains about the work, the customers, her tips...

I wish these idiots...

They're idiots now?

Now? Where have you been Art? They've always been idiots and I wish they...

What?

I wish they knew the old fifteen percent rule. Unfortunately none of them know how to tip. The best I do these days is ten percent. A person can hardly live on fifteen percent, much less ten percent. I'm dying in this job.

Then get a new one. You could work anywhere you want.

Oh? And how would I manage that? Remember I don't even have a diploma.

But you have experience. You have tons of experience.

That and arch support will get you nowhere fast in today's economy. Believe you me, Art. And I would appreciate it if you figured out how to talk to me without belittling me.

Can I have another coffee?

Are you going to tip me?

Fifteen percent.

All right, then, you can have another coffee. But some folks come in here sit all day drinking my coffee and walk out leaving two dollars to cover the cup of coffee, no tip included.

Don't worry about it Rita. Things are bound to improve. It's only an unlucky streak is all.

But I'm tired of being unlucky. All day I watch people come and go and I can't help feel they're all luckier than me.

That's not true and you know it.

It is true, Art. They get to come and go as they please but I'm stuck working all day in this shithole going nowhere fast.

You have me.

Like I say, I'm unlucky. And I did nothing to deserve it.

Smile honey. A smile is the beginning of a winning streak, I promise you.

She looks at me like she wants to kill me, then she crosses her eyes and sticks out her tongue.

I'm sorry, Rita.

It's OK.

I love you, Rita.

I love you too, I suppose.

No supposing about it.

No, let me suppose, Art. It's all I have. It's my fifteen percent margin, this supposing.

Rita, hang in there. Business is bound to upturn. I promise.

You and your promises, Art. That's all you have are promises. But you never seem able to deliver.

I look at my watch and smile at Rita.

Well, darling...

Well?

Am I going to see you tonight?

Not tonight, Art.

Oh, come on baby.

I don't feel like it tonight. I'm sorry, Art. I'm tired.

Come on over. I'll rub your feet and spread mentholated ointment on your calves.

I've got to go home, Art. Take care of my cats. Get my mail. That sort of thing. Pay the bills. How about you spend a few days alone and think about this?

What's there to think about?

I'll give you a few days to come up with an answer to that.

Until then...

Until then you're on your own.

•

I walk out the door and buy a loaf of Wonder Bread at the corner store. I head for the park where I feed the pigeons. I find a bench near the fountain and already the birds are coming from everywhere to gather round me. They know me by sight, these birds. They're pretty smart. Either that or I have them well-trained. Dog walkers pass on either side, kids on skateboards, office workers loaded down with satchels carrying their laptops stride past me like I'm crazy.

It's the least I can do, feed these birds.

Everything else I've managed to botch up, but taking care of these birds. It's the least I can do.

I'm one of those who never had anything against pigeons. Everybody hates them. Then they hate crows. Then they hate the common grackle. In that order. The problem with pigeons, they'll tell you, is that pigeons are dirty filthy birds. Flying rats. The problem with crows, they'll tell you, is that crows are raucous birds that make too much noise and are generally just pests, and the problem with grackles is that they raid the nests and eat the young of other species.

A bird is a bird to me. I don't hate them. What's there to hate? They're animals that manage to get along in the city and survive. It seems admirable to me. The idea of judging a bird for how it chooses to get along is a bit ludicrous. Judging people on the other hand, seems OK. People are open game. I like birds because they're not people. I don't find birds particularly dirty. I often find people to be dirty, or if not dirty, unpleasant in ways that suggest they are dirty. Pigeons and sparrows possess their own wonder and beauty and it's not so hard to see if you only look. I don't mind feeding pigeons and sparrows even if they are common. Who am I to turn my nose up at a bird because it happens to be common? I'm common. What's wrong with common? I see a friend in these birds. They gather around me when I feed them. They swoop down from the tree tops and they accept my offerings with gratitude. I try to cluck like them. I give them names and try to recognize them from feeding to feeding. Bernie or Tweet or Apple or Broken Toe or Split Wing. It gives me pleasure to name the birds and peace of mind to feed them.

I didn't think I'd be one of those people—bird people—and in particular a person who feeds pigeons and sparrows. For the longest time I was always zipping around. My life was too busy to consider the birds. When I was too busy, I thought them dirty and pesky like everyone else. But now I have more time and I see the beauty of these ordinary city birds. I toss the pieces of Wonder Bread into the sky. The pigeons can swoop down from the trees and gather the bread in their beaks before the bread hits the ground. The grace and skill and beauty of this is sometimes too much for me. It's the sort of thing that makes me grateful to still be alive. I don't always feel that gratitude, but sitting in the park, tossing torn bread slices to the pigeons and sparrows fills my soul with gratitude.

There are dog walkers in the park, and a few lovers sitting on the bench across from me. I had that sort of love with Adeleine but never had it with Rita. I probably won't have that type of love again. Love is for the young. Love is for the unwounded. Love is for someone else. I don't know how to love any more. I'm a private eye whose business is slowly disappearing into oblivion and I could care less. I can't even build up the energy to swoop down from the treetops, like the pigeons, and gather the few breadcrumbs that are tossed to me

After feeding the birds I go back to the office to see if there's anything going on. Wanda is long gone. I can't believe how meticulously clean my office is. Ever since Adeleine was gunned down, Wanda has been obsessed with keeping it hospital clean. The phone rings. I pick up. A voice on the other end suggesting business.

Triple A Detective AAAgency...

Triple A what?

Detective AAAgency. Can I help you.

Is this the plumber?

The plumber?

Is this Triple AAA Plumbing?

No, I say, it's the detective agency. Do you. Would you like to contract a detective?

It's plumbing. I need a plumber.

Before I can get another word out to try and lure this voice into my business, the phone goes dead.

⊙

As I said before, prior to becoming a detective, I had worked for nearly two decades as an anonymous cog in a large telecom business.

All I was there was a clerk in a large office building. I was a waterboy always running to get water for some higher-up who was thirsty. I would read inventory reports on antiquated computers. Huge reports that took all day to read. It was terribly dull work on a green screen with a cursor prompt. Then there were better computers with better programs, and a chunk of my work went away. Then my company went under, and let me tell you it happened faster than I thought these things could happen. One day we were a healthy company, the next week we were filing for Chapter 11 bankruptcy, and I was out on my ear looking for another job. You know how they say: the rug was pulled out from under me? Well it was literally like that. The rug had been pulled out. I had been called into the HR office, and an HR personnel explained the situation to me.

The HR personnel pointed out that the new computer programs could handle the majority of my job, and so it made sense from the company's point of view to eliminate my job. The HR personnel was very sorry to inform me of the restructuring but there was nothing to be done to keep me on. I was given a check to fill out my pay period and told to go home.

HR smiled, then frowned. I frowned, then smiled. I gathered my check. I was polite. How could I not be polite? I knew it hurt the HR personnel more than it hurt me, at least until it didn't hurt the HR personnel. That was at the moment the door closed behind me.

When I stood in the parking lot trying to get my bearings, something unexpected happened: my legs gave out and I collapsed on the asphalt pavement. I had never before been fired from a job. How was I going to tell my wife? What was I going to tell my daughter? What would I tell myself? That I had been fired? That I was one of the losers in the faltering economy? Only be patient Mr. Topp, the HR personnel told me, and you *will* find a foothold—a new foothold. You did valuable work for us, Mr. Topp. You were an integral member of our team. If you are patient, I am certain you will go on to be an integral member of someone else's team.

HR pushed the cream-colored check forward across the desk. I reached for it. I turned and stepped out the door. Then I collapsed in the parking lot. I thought I was having a heart attack or a brain aneurysm or both. One minute everything was fine. The next moment, the rug was pulled out from under me. I was disoriented by a world spinning faster than I could keep up. Then I collapsed.

At first, I didn't have the courage to tell Adeleine I'd lost my job. I felt guilty. I felt like my nuts had been cut off. I felt that I was a lion who no longer was able to go in for the kill. It was a ridiculous analogy because all I was was inventory control, but that's how I felt. Then there was that image. I couldn't shake it from my mind. I had collapsed on the asphalt, so my face was pressed in the hot tar and gravel, the world spinning out of control, and there was literally nothing I could do about it for what seemed like an eternity: the hot sun beating down, though I know it was only for a few moments. What caused me to collapse like that? I started to cry compulsively. I couldn't control it. I cried for the memory of my mother and father whom I tried to do right by. I cried for my wife and my daughter, Meg. Most of all I cried for myself, and when I couldn't cry any more, I passed out.

A moment later I was alert again. I shook my leg and pushed myself up off the pavement. I stumbled to my car, unlocked the door, and got in. I found a handkerchief and tried to wipe my face clean; it was smeared black with tar. I fumbled with the keys and when the ignition took, I drove slowly out of the parking lot. I felt my shirt pocket for the cream-colored check. It was still there. I drove around until I found myself in a church parking lot. I slowed the car to a stop and walked across a field to a stand of trees. There was a bend in the Des Plaines River. I walked through the woods and sat on a grass knoll overlooking the river. I sat there for some time just watching the river flow by. I was wondering if I should kill myself. I hardly saw the point of going on. This would be the spot to do it. If only I had my Ruger on me, I could solve this problem.

Eventually I made my way home, and after showering to clean myself off, I found myself slightly dazed at the dinner table with Adeleine and Meg, eating one of Adeleine's fabulous home-cooked meals as if nothing at all were amiss. I was dipping the fatty end of a steak into her beef gravy and using the napkin to wipe sweat off my brow.

How was your day, honey? my wife asked.

Excellent. How was yours?

Well...I sold a $2.5 million dollar house today in Bucktown to a wealthy young couple. He's corporate law at some big firm. She's high-level management in corporate finance—if that's what you want to know...

At that precise moment I should have told her that I'd been canned from the telecom business and therefore I was a nothing and a nobody and she shouldn't waste any more of her time on me. But I was still in a state of shock, so I passed on the personal commentary and merely forked a bloody piece of steak into my mouth and smiled at her.

Congratulations! I said. This calls for a bottle of champagne.

After that, we poured a bit of champagne and toasted her success. That night I fell asleep dreaming of vultures picking my pockets.

•

For the next two weeks, I didn't have the heart to tell Adeleine I had been fired. I didn't have the heart for any of it: for being fired, for finding a new foothold. I was a naïf. I should have been better at what I did at the telecom business. I see that now, but at the time, I was blind to my own deficiencies. I should have been more proactive. I should have been more adroit at playing office politics. I should have smiled more often. I was a sour puss. I said it like it was. I didn't sugarcoat the truth. I sat in meetings and spoke my mind regardless of whether or not I made enemies. I was a problem solver. I was hell-bent on solving our company's problems such as I construed them. Later, I came to see that I had misconstrued what the company's problems were, and therefore I had spoken my mind contrary to what the real problems in the organization were, which made my bosses look bad.

Then I became a problem, which became glaringly obvious after the Chapter 11 filing when the HR personnel fired me.

In the interim period between when I'd been fired and when I told my wife I'd been fired, I left for work every morning as if I still had a job, but rather than going to work, I went to the racetrack with Cal. Or Cal and I went shooting guns at the range. Or I went fishing by myself on the Des Plaines River for carp. I was trying to regain control of something I had lost, but I didn't know what I had lost. I might say I lost my entire identity. I didn't know who I was any more, nor did I know what would become of me. I feared what would become of me. I went from a man who was filled with confidence to a failure who was fearful of every little thing. One day, after losing several hundred dollars at the track, I decided it was time to tell my wife what had happened.

I explained that I had lost my job. I was collateral damage. I used those exact words to explain my situation. I was collateral damage of the collapsing economy. I told her about the cream-colored check, which was a laughably small amount.

After that money runs out, I said, if I don't have a new job I don't know what will happen to me.

You know we don't need to worry about money, she said. Take your time, Art. Find a job that you are interested in. Be patient. Now is a wonderful opportunity for you. Now is your time to define for yourself. Go out once and for all and find out who it is you want to be.

I want to be me, I told her.

Then be you, Art. Be the best *you* you can be. Our cash situation is such that there is absolutely no pressure. And if you're wondering if I still love you...

Yes...

I do.

•

But there was pressure, because there was nothing I wanted to be. I certainly didn't want to get fired again from an HR personnel. Nor, for that matter, was I eager to try to win a job from another HR personnel. I took my payout and I filed for and collected unemployment, and I drove around for months looking for new work. I had headhunters working for me.

Adeleine suggested teaching, and I laughed at her without even giving it a second thought.

Then one day, I was at an interview at another telecom, and I got into an argument over whether or not I thought I could use the computer programs available to advance the business in the direction to which it needed advancing.

What direction is that? I asked. I still had a chip on my shoulder, and it showed. North, South, East or West?

Are you serious, Mr. Topp?

Yes.

With that I stood up with both of my fuck-off fingers flung high, and I walked out the door of another HR personnel's office.

Then I was driving in my car when I started asking myself serious questions apropos Adeleine's conversations with me: if I did change my career, what would it be? In fact, it was a friend who had gotten me into the telecom industry. I was always going the path of least resistance. But now, driving in my car, I thought: if I were to take matters into my own hands and be anything I want to be, what would I do? I felt pathetic that I couldn't come up with an answer. I thought about it for a long time but nothing ever entered my head. Then one thing led to another and I got to thinking about my education.

I had never had much of an education. You know they say education is wasted on the young. Well to a certain extent I would say this was true for me, and I was feeling lousy that I hadn't tried to do more with myself, education-wise. But suddenly there was something that jumped out at me from those days: an almost inane conversation I had had ages ago at Steinmetz high school on the northwest side of Chicago where I had been a student.

My high school experience at Steinmetz was generally unpleasant, and it didn't offer much in the way of an education, but I trod on with it best I could. To give you an idea, the famous Las Vegas mobster, Tony "The Ant" Spilotro, had been a student at Steinmetz the generation before me. And he and his brother Michael were beaten in a Bensenville basement by mobsters, then killed and buried six feet under an Indiana cornfield only a few years after I graduated from Steinmetz. In fact, when I attended the school, there were still a bunch of little Tony Spilotro types running around its corridors. Some of these guys were my friends. I lifted weights with them. I slammed my fists into punching bags with them. I shot guns with them. I even terrorized other students with them. As to my studies, like I say, there wasn't much to it. However, I can vividly recall one day sitting around the lunch table with my friends when a fellow classmate, Terrence MacDonald, told us about his dad. His dad was a detective. He was a private eye. I didn't think much about Terrance, who we nicknamed alternately 'Big Mac' and 'Had A Farm.' But Terrance said something about his dad that stuck in my head. He said: My dad likes the detective business because it gives him time to watch the horses and fish.

So after that interview, I was sitting in my car at a stoplight waiting for the light to turn green. Maybe I was humming that nursery rhyme, Old MacDonald, or maybe I was singing the Big Mac jingle. But that conversation with Terrance from so long ago just drifted up from wherever I had kept it—drifted right into plain view, and there it was. I don't know why this sentence of Terrence's stuck in my head, but it did. I honestly never forgot it. It was just something I carried with me. Why not become a detective? I thought. I like to watch the horses and fish. What's more, there are worse jobs out there. Besides, I'm sure I'm capable of doing it. Then the light turned green, and I drove off to tell Adeleine.

◉

I don't know what made me think I would be capable of being a private eye. I suppose I just imagined that anyone with half a brain could do it. But I was wrong about this. I never quite figured the business out. I was probably not meant to be a private eye. In fact, I was probably more suited to being a cog in a big organization. But because there was a war between me and HR personnel, I had officially given that up. I was going my own way. Starting fresh. I was going to self-determine who I was going to be from here on out. What do you want to do? I want to be a private eye.

When I proposed the detective idea to Adeleine as a way to regain my foothold in the economy, she outright laughed at me because she thought I was joking. When I insisted that I wasn't joking, she grew serious, frowned a little, and said it was a bad idea. She didn't think I had what it took to succeed in such a business. She knew that I was inclined to laziness, and so I was probably better working in a job with a boss. With a boss telling me what to do, I would be fine, but as a boss, my laziness would get the better of me. But if I didn't want to go back into something like telecom, she thought my skills— 'Your skills' is what she said—could be better applied in a career like teaching. What's more, she said—and this she argued time and time again until I finally earned my detective license and hung my shingle, at which point she stopped arguing with me—what's more, not only will you be ineffectual as a detective, and as your own boss, but as a result you will find it a dull and uninteresting career change.

In the end, Adeleine proved correct on every point. After hanging my shingle—and I hung it on my wife's dime—I knew almost immediately that not only was I not suited for such a job, but that it really wasn't a very interesting job. Perhaps it was just my disposition that made me think it wasn't an interesting job. If I had been suited for the work in the first place, I might have felt differently. Indeed I might have found it a fascinating business.

However, I did not find it fascinating. It was an albatross around my neck.

What's worse, once I took the business on I didn't know how to back out of it. I didn't know how to cry uncle. I was in whole-hog as they say, and I was too stubborn to budge out.

Furthermore, I found that the secondary benefits of being a self-employed detective—the fishing, the horses, the shooting of the guns at the shooting range— were not distracting enough to keep me from worrying that I had made a terrible life choice and that my life, as a result, was being squandered. Going to the horses or fishing only enhanced the sense that I was making a terrible mistake and that wasted time and life was the only outcome I could expect from such foolishness. Yet rain, sleet, snow, or shine: off to the horses I went, or fishing, or shooting my guns at the shooting range with Cal.

When I did get some business and my wife was killed as a direct result of my work, I realized that becoming a detective had been the most fateful and devastating decision I had ever made, and I never got over the whimsical stupidity of my own thinking.

•

The hardest thing, I tell Cal.

We're at the horses. Or we're shooting. Or we're in the car going hither and thither.

God damn it, he says, pounding on his horn.

You're too aggressive a driver.

I can't help it, Cal shouts back at me. These stupid drivers!

They're not all stupid. It's just that...

It's just what?

Like I was saying before you interrupted me. The hardest thing about all this...

About what?

About my wife being dead.

Cal looks across the seat at me with a touch of fear in his eyes. A look that says: Oh shit, he's going to start talking about his dead wife.

I have to talk about my dead wife to someone. Who can I go to if not you? I ask Cal.

Yeah, but you have Rita to spill your heart to. Remember, I'm just some guy you shoot guns with.

I can't talk to Rita about this. She doesn't even know how Adeleine died.

She doesn't know? How can she not know?

I've never had the courage to tell her.

Well you got to tell her, Art, it's been five years. And how long have you guys been going together?

Almost as long.

That's what I thought. And you haven't told her?

No.

He slams the steering wheel with the palm of his hand and laughs in incredulity.

How can she not know how your wife died, Art? And I thought I was non-communicative. I thought I had a hard time opening up. Art you *have* to tell Rita how your wife died.

You don't understand, I tell him. She doesn't want to talk about Adeleine.

What does she want to talk about?

Anything but.

Why would she, I suppose.

Exactly. Why would she, and to be honest, I don't blame her.

I suppose I wouldn't either.

I also worry if I told her she'd just think I was feeling sorry for myself.

Why would she think that?

I don't know.

We drive on.

Can you slow it down a little? I ask him when the car veers into the gravel around a bend in the road.

No problem, Art. The thing is. I want to get to the range and start shooting. I promised my mom I'd be home in time to take her shopping.

What time did you say?

That I'd be back by seven.

That gives us forty-five minutes, Cal. Hardly enough time. You may as well turn around.

Nonsense. Forty-five minutes is plenty of time. No need to turn around now. We're almost there.

At the gun range, he pulls his Uzi out of its case and starts unloading it full-auto at a paper target. *BLURT. BLURT. BLURT.* He shreds the target. I press the electric switch and bring it back and change targets.

He leans into his gun and his eyes crunch in focus and a small grin hangs in the corner of his mouth as he lets go again with that damn Uzi. He shoots that thing like he's one with it, like it's an extension of him. It's the only time I see him entirely at ease with himself. His body vibrates and shakes with recoil, but his focus remains unfazed. It's at moments like this when I feel an almost inexplicable admiration for the man.

It's my turn. I step into the lane, unpack my pussy gun, my .22 with the suppressor. I take aim and go: *Pop. Pop. Pop.* And what I aim at I invariably miss.

It's his turn. He steps forward and off he goes again. *BLURT. BLURT. BLURT.* And again, *BLURT. BLURT. BLURT.* We put another target out and he shoots it down.

God that feels good, he says stepping back from position and letting me come forward. What a stress reliever.

Now my turn: *Pop. Pop. Pop.*

You have stress. What kind of stress can you possibly have, Cal?

I change the target and we fire off another series of rounds.

My mom stresses me out. Not having a job stresses me out.

BLURT. BLURT. BLURT.

But this makes me feel a world better.

I should have your problems

Pop. Pop. Pop.

What problems do you have, Art? You've got a woman.

BLURT. BLURT. BLURT.

Yeah, and what's your point?

Pop. Pop. Pop.

Well, it's more than I ever had. So count your blessings and stop complaining.

I offer to change the target, but Cal flags me away.

Not necessary, buddy, he shouts. Then he goes again. *BLURT. BLURT. BLURT.* Shredding the target this way and that until there is nothing left but a few tattered pieces hanging and a pile of shell casings at his feet.

Ah, wonderful, he says packing up his Uzi. Nothing like it. I feel a million times better.

Then we hop in his car and he drives like nuts to get home to his mom by seven.

He drops me off and smiles. Thanks for coming out old buddy, he says, slapping me on the back. I grab my gun and barely have time to get the door closed before he's off at full speed to his mom.

•

When Cal disappears around the corner, I feel exhausted all of a sudden. I unlock the door to my place. I can't believe Adeleine is dead. That's the whole point. It's not just the dying that gets you. It's the fact that they stay dead. That's what I can't abide. Even after all these years I keep expecting her to show up any minute. I keep walking into my place expecting her to suddenly be there. The whole problem with this thing is she was taken away so abruptly I can't believe she's gone, and now I feel all I do is wait for her to return even though I know in my heart of hearts that she never will.

It's this not being in a routine, I tell myself. That's what's gotten the better of me. There's something not right with me. There's been something not right with me for so long I don't even remember when things were right for me. Whenever I try to remember back to a time in my life that was normal I always go back to my life with Adeleine. Adeleine is my Eden. My eighteen-year marriage to Adeleine was my heaven. I'm afraid to say I've been kicked out of Eden with her death and I don't know if I'll ever be able to return.

Since I've been kicked out of Eden I've been searching for a routine. At night if Rita and I aren't together, I head on down to Murphy's. It's the only bar I ever go to. I know just about everyone in the bar. I don't consider myself a regular at Murphy's just because I know there are problems once you start admitting these kinds of things to yourself. You are better off telling yourself you are not a regular, even though you go to the bar on a regular occasion, than you are admitting you're a regular. I like not being a regular, even though I come here all the time. For one, by not being a regular I can always say to myself: at least my life is not so lonesome I have to spend it night after night in a bar, like these guys. At least I'm not like all of these guys.

I like coming to this bar because it is a nice comfortable place. What's more there's a steady stream of women who come in because across the street is a theater and often women will come in after the show for a drink and it's a nice place to be if you want to see new faces from time to time. Occasionally I talk to one or another of the women. I smile. I try to be happy. I try to imagine if this is the place I'll find my next one. That is, if things go south between me and Rita.

The other night, for instance, there was this woman who stepped into Murphy's. She was a sparkling soul. I don't remember the last time I saw a woman so full of energy and life, such a light, and here she was swimming into Murphy's. I even bought her a drink, and then she was gone, just like that. One drink, a bit of small talk, and then she was gone into the night never to be seen by me again. A stain on my memory. A bit of brightness. And where...where did she go?

•

One night some guy is sitting next to me talking my ear off. He's a bouncer who follows strippers around on their jaunts. He's telling me about one, and as I listen I order up another round of beers.

He says: There's this one woman I drive around, her name is Flower.

Do you pack a gun?

No. I don't pack a gun. I wish I could, some of the scrapes I get in, but I don't pack a gun. It's safer that way, believe it or not. I want to intimidate, but not hurt.

I could see that, I say, buying him a beer. It's more dangerous that way, though.

Yes. More dangerous. But it's the price you pay if you want to be righteous.

That's the term he used: Righteous.

Absolutely, I say, clinking his beer and tipping it back. To righteousness.

Anyway, this woman, Flower. The things she can do with her cunt. By the way, do you do pills?

No.

Codeine, he says, pulling a couple of pills out of his front pocket.

No, you go right on ahead.

He takes his pills and washes them down with his beer.

Anyway this stripper—Flower, her name is—she shoves all kinds of stuff in her twat. I once saw her stick a lit bong up her pussy and inhale.

Where did the smoke come out?

Can you believe it? She made it come out her ass! He laughs. Anyway, as a follow up to this, she likes to stuff her pussy with pickles. Those sweet little gherkin types. And then you know what she does?

What?

She tells the guys at the party to gather around and get a good look at what they paid to see. She spreads her legs; she takes aim and shoots 'em one at a time at different guys in the room. And they shoot out, bang, just like that.

They shoot out?

Just like that. She tells me she aims for the whites of their eyes. She hates men. That's what she says. That was her complaint, night after night. How much she hated her job stripping for men. She hated stripping. She hated men. So how did she solve her problem? She shot at them with pickles pushed from her twat. It made her happy. It gave her relief.

If she didn't like men, then why did she strip for them?

Cash money of course. But I'm telling you this. Had she a real gun and not pickles, had her gun been real, I guarantee you. She wouldn't have thought twice about using it and killing every man that felt he had to see her up close like that. She hated them. Meanest person I ever saw naked, but with her clothes on she was really quite friendly.

But she, too, didn't have a gun...

Yes. And I suppose in that way, she too was righteous.

•

Some nights, Rita appears through the doors, finds me here and drags me home. She can't stand to see me hanging out at this place. She calls everyone who drinks here losers. She calls it a loser bar and drags me out of there like I don't belong here but then she calls me a loser.

You're a loser, Art. I can't believe I care about a guy like you.

You don't have to care about a guy like me if you don't want to. No one is forcing you.

There you go again. I'm half-tempted to leave you right now.

Then why don't you?

Because to be honest with you, Art, I'm holding out for something...

What's that?

I'm holding out for you to finally getting around to being truthful.

I am truthful.

You're a sack of shit is what you are...but as pertains to the truth, you're a far way from it buddy.

And how might I get closer, if you don't mind me asking?

You might get closer by telling me how the hell your wife died.

You know how my wife died.

In fact, I don't.

I told you it was an accident. She died in an accident.

And what kind of accident might that have been? There are all sorts of accidents.

An *accident* accident...As far as I can tell there is only one type. And that's what she died of.

You're a fool, Art, for not being truthful to me.

I am talking truthful.

You're drunk is what you are. One day though, I hope we can revisit this conversation.

•

I suppose I should be grateful that Rita cares so much for me, but having her show up and drag me home from Murphy's is disconcerting and embarrassing. I'm a man, goddamn it, and if I want to spend my night at the bar getting soused, goddamn it, well then let me spend it at the bar.

You said you needed time alone to visit with your cats and do your mail. No need to drag me home.

And yet when she does this, everybody at the bar sits there, watching. I know what they're wondering. They're wondering how it is a guy ends up in this state— out for a drink, and then the girlfriend arrives and drags him home. They're hoping that it'll never happen to them, never, not in a million years, so help them God, it'll never happen their woman showing up unannounced come to make fools of them and drag them home.

Rita usually shows up unannounced—which is the embarrassment of the whole situation.

Anyway, there I'll be at Murphy's minding my own business having a conversation with someone or another like Eddy, the bartender who is the guy who owns the place. Eddy's no businessman, but somehow or another he's done OK by this bar. It's a mystery that both baffles me and attracts me. I have my business, which is failing, but Eddy has his bar that he does well by. I'm curious how someone can have a business and be anything other than a failure. But he has a strategy that I've come to admire. Between the regulars and the theater crowd, he does OK, and there's something about him that I admire. Something hard to put my finger on. He goes about his business day after day just as I do, but he gets by, whereas I'm always wondering when I'm going to hit the bottom of the pit. He gets things done in his own way and he ends up being successful, and who knows how I'll end up? I keep hoping for the best but in this life, at least, there are no guarantees.

I'll be talking to Eddy about guns because Eddy, like Cal, is a bit of a gun nut. I'll tell him about Cal's Uzi or about my Ruger. Eddy likes to hunt big game. I myself have never gotten into hunting, but it's interesting listening to him talk about some caribou or something that he'd taken down with a bolt-action .308 Winchester Model 70 from two hundred and fifty yards out. A fly-in camp near the Arctic Circle, no less, and the trekking across spongy tundra and the big sky filled with waterfowl and distance in all directions like nothing he's ever seen and the great wash of fast moving rivers across gravel and the brown bears like spots on the horizon that you would peer at through your scope to get a better look and nighttime in a flimsy tent listening to the noises outside and the aurora borealis that was so beautiful he named his kid after it.

The way Eddy talked it would take you away to a different place, and one morning two hundred yards outside his tent he saw a small gathering of caribou cows and some juveniles and fifty yards yet further out there was a big bull standing all by himself sniffing the air with his nostrils then dropping his head to nibble a bit at the tundra and then came the scramble for the Winchester as Eddy tried for the shot of his life and he felt the throb of heart in his head as he tried to steady the gun and there it was the big bull with the massive rack jerking around the inside of Eddy's scope and then the gentle squeeze of the trigger and Eddy got him straight through the carotid artery first the bullet hit the bull then almost in slow motion the caribou turned its head around as if scanning the horizon for something—that peaceful, curious look animals get—almost human on its face—a human with horns—and then as if it had been detonated from within the bull collapsed like a building—*boom*—hitting the turf and then they had to call the fly-in plane and while waiting, there was the cleaning of the caribou and the eating raw of the nearly-still-beating heart. Just then the door opens and to my surprise it's Rita come to claim me while Eddy is mid-sentence and holy shit why me because I want to know what happens next.

Hi Art, she says, grabbing my arm.

Hi Rita.

Time to go, Art.

One more drink and then let's go, OK?

No. I want you out of here now, OK?

OK, I say. For what other choice do I have but to say OK and goodnight Eddy?

Goodnight Art.

Nice talking with you as always, Eddy.

Same same, Art.

By the way, how was the heart?

The heart?

The caribou's heart? You said you ate it raw?

And before he can answer Rita's tugging at my arm.

I don't want to listen to this.

And how do you do it, I yell into the place, as she drags me out. I scream into the place as she drags me out: How do you, Eddy? How do you run a successful business and live a successful life? Tell me how do you to it? I need to know!

Shut up you crazy drunk, Rita says, pulling on my arm and dragging away. You're talking stupid.

Off Rita and I go, off into the night. With her shouting: Truthful, truthful, I need you to be truthful, Art.

Truthful about what, Rita?

Truthful about what you've become.

What have I become, Rita?

You've become a loser, Art, just like all the rest. And tell me, what would your daughter Meg think if she saw you like this?

What if?

Yeah, Art, what if?

•

The crowd at Albert Volares' funeral is getting antsy.

The kid in the pink housecoat steps away from the gathering and sits on a tombstone with a girl who has long blond hair that blows in the breeze. Another boy stands in front of her.

The one kid in the housecoat tilts his head upward, and the girl pushes the hair from her face and looks at the dirt near her feet. The other looks off in the direction of the priest. They seem nonchalant. Disconnected. Sculptures to eternally disaffected youth. Some way to get out of school, witnessing the grief of others. I feel I don't understand them. I feel born of a different generation.

The mother of the deceased, on the other hand, I know what she's going through. I understand what I'm seeing there. She is trying mightily to keep from breaking down. Her husband stands behind her and grips her around the waist trying to keep her from exploding. The priest speaks in a monotone as if he's done this thing a million times before, which he probably has.

Albert was a good boy, the priest says. Now he is an angel in heaven. He was an altar boy who helped serve communion. Now he is an angel in heaven. It is in communion that we are gathered here today to put Albert to rest. Let us pray that his life was not in vain. Some of us are given to living long lives, others of us, the Lord will take before our time, but it is not incumbent on us to divine the Lord's will. It is only enough to understand that the Lord has a will and a plan for each of us and it is his will that we pray, may be done.

⊙

After that Italian dinner when we first met, Rita and I wandered into the hotel across from my office. We took a room on the thirteenth floor. Neither of us had bags, and the fact that we found ourselves here, going up in an elevator, astonished me a little. It's funny the curveballs life can throw you. One minute you're throwing flowers on your wife's grave. The next moment you're going up an elevator with a strange woman you just drank too much Chianti with.

I never do this sort of thing, she said.

Neither do I.

I hope you know I don't normally do this sort of thing.

No need to apologize.

I never do this.

Neither do I.

I'm not so easy as this. It's only...

Listen I've been married forever. It's new to me too. Nothing to worry about.

It's only that I. You have been a real comfort to me today. I want to thank you.

She wore just the faintest perfume that was slightly alienating.

I tried to ease the situation with a smile.

It's OK to try something different. We only live once.

Yes, isn't this what this is about?

What do you mean?

About living once. We met in a cemetery. This is about life, living, the recognition that we...that we live once and then we die.

OK...

She paused, took a breath. What are we going to do in this hotel room anyway?

I suppose we'll just have to go into the hotel room and find out. By the way, let me say it again, that's a nice sweater.

My mom knit it.

She must have been something.

She understood me.

I'm sure that was nice.

For me, it was everything.

The elevator binged and we got off.

•

She sat down on the bed and I sat in a chair across from her.

How have you been since your wife died?

How have I been? Terrible.

But do you feel like I feel?

I don't know.

You don't know how you feel?

A little. And I suppose I don't know how you feel.

Alone is how I feel.

I do too, I suppose. Though I have a daughter. And my office is across the street. And I know lots of people so I don't feel quite so alone.

What's her name?

Who, my daughter?

Yeah.

Meg. She's down in New Orleans. Tulane. We sorted through a bunch of things after the funeral and then abruptly, she left. And so she's there and I'm here. But yes. I don't feel alone so much as...

What.

Uprooted. Broken. Hurt. Unable to go on...Shall I go on? I feel disoriented. Lost. I don't have much desire for anything.

They say it will pass.

I hope so.

It will pass.

I don't know. Maybe it will. Maybe it won't. We'll see.

•

An El train catching orange hues of light rattled the tracks outside our window. I saw a blur of passengers on the train flickering by. They were packed in, standing room only, plugged into their headsets or looking blankly ahead. Rita and I sat there for a while talking. The late afternoon sunlight was filtering through a south-facing window throwing a trapezoid of light across the edge of the bed, lighting her lap, and falling across the floor. I sat in the shadows near a bureau looking at her and she was lovely, really, and vulnerable, and I could tell she knew as little about these things as I did. It was as if we sat there trying to assimilate not only to the reality of our new losses but to the reality of each other, to the reality of this new person right here in front of me; I was taking in this three-dimensional flesh and blood breathing human being who was stranded on the scabrous shoals of the planet just as I was and who still wanted to take a stab at what new adventures life might have in store.

She was a stranger really, and in some ways she has never stopped being a stranger to me, just as I must seem a perpetual stranger to her. She is some combination of signs and signals that I have never been fully able to interpret and understand. Even then I felt her frequency was tuned for a different receiver, and yet I felt it was incumbent upon me to discover that frequency nevertheless, and understand it as if what it were transmitting were meant for me, and not someone else.

We sat there in a not quite comfortable silence. I didn't know what to say or do next. We had made it this far without thinking about it, but suddenly *thought* kicked in, and self-consciousness and worry, and that wonder that had gathered about us as we had sat on the tombstone sorting out our separate losses disappeared, and I felt tricked. Who was this person? Why were we here? Why should we do anything next? Why not just turn around and go back to our loss, where we belong, to the life we had before the moment we first saw each other on the tombstone?

Why not turn around and go back, I wanted to say. And I could tell as she sat there across from me that she wanted to say something of the sort as well. Something along the lines of, maybe this wasn't a good idea after all. Listen, we're both adults here.

We've already got plenty of water that has flowed beneath our respective bridges. No need worrying about saving face, no need worrying about admitting a mistake. Can we just say that this is probably not the right time to be doing this? Can we just part ways and say: thanks for lunch; it was nice meeting you? If you ever want to meet again, don't hesitate to call.

Instead we just sat there. Our eyes diverted. I looked occasionally at her and felt an inexplicable sense of compassion for her. I wanted to hug her and say I was sorry for everything. If it were Adeleine, I would have said I was sorry for everything...

I'm sorry my dear.

Sorry for what, honey? I'm dead. I no longer care for sorry.

Sorry for everything. I am so goddamned sorry for everything in the world that I have ever done to you.

No need saying sorry for anything, Art. Really, you were wonderful. The light of my life. I don't regret a thing.

•

So Rita and I just sat there not saying a word. And before I knew what I was doing, I walked over. I sat down next her and I put my arm around her shoulder. It was a bonier shoulder than Adeleine's. She seemed made of bird bones by comparison—easily snappable.

She sat there neither accommodating me nor disallowing me. So we sat a moment like this, and suddenly she turned her head into my shoulder and I brought her close to me in an embrace.

I'm sorry, I said to her, not knowing what else to do or say.

For what?

And it was true, she had a point. What could I possibly be sorry for? We were both consenting adults. We were both here of our own volition, and so I said: For your loss.

She said, very sweetly: I'm sorry for yours.

Thank you.

Now can you promise to do me a favor, Art?

Anything.

Whatever happens, never, don't ever, say sorry again. Do you understand that?

Deal. With that she lifted her face to mine and we lay down together on the bed.

•

The first time Adeleine and I slept together happened years earlier. It was just after she graduated from Northwestern. We had met only days earlier at a party, and then we ran into each other unexpectedly again at a grocery store. We had coffee, and afterwards she told me to call her. I waited a day or two, and when I called, she picked up the phone, and without asking me how I was doing, merely suggested I come over to her house. She was still living with her parents in Winnetka. We were only twenty-two years old at the time. As old as Meg is now.

I was never one of those guys growing up who would bed his girlfriend at her parents' house. I prided myself on having better options—like the car, or some place deep in the forest preserves on a blanket and a bed of leaves—but the house Adeleine grew up in was actually pretty nice. Her parents were out of town for the month, so there was no chance they would suddenly barge in on us. The house was a modernist box perched on a slight grade overlooking a precipitous ravine with woods and a little stream running along the bottom. They had modernist stuff on the walls, modernist furniture. Minimalist this and that. All clean lines. Off-white cream-colored walls, floors that disappeared into the night beyond the windows.

Like Cal, I was a guy who grew up in a bungalow on the northwest side, which, when growing up, was paradise enough for me. So I didn't envy her wealth at the time, and that probably meant something to her.

I enjoyed my life. I found if you liked your life it didn't matter where you came from. Liking life was the key to success. So many people caught up in the chase for money—but it was terribly misdirected. Money never made anyone happy, but figuring out how to be happy and stay happy—this was success.

•

I had many conversations at the track with Cal about this.

What's the best thing in the world? I would ask.

Pussy.

After pussy?

Tits.

After tits?

Beer.

After beer?

Money.

After money?

More pussy.

And around and around we went, but one day I asked Cal a different question.

What about the guy who is locked up in solitary confinement and he can't get these things you're talking about. What would be the best thing to him?

Pornography.

Come on, seriously.

A bit of light...

But if he didn't have light?

A bit of food...

But if he didn't have food?

A piece of chalk to scratch against the wall...

And if he didn't have that?

Then he'd have to learn how to be happy with what he has—because he sure ain't got a hell of a lot. Who is this guy, anyways? Someone you know doing solitary confinement?

It's just a hypothetical question about happiness is all...

You want happiness Art?

Hypothetically, I suppose I do.

It doesn't have to be hypothetical, Art. I mean, look at me. Who am I? I'm your friend Cal, and most people looking on would say: What a lousy life that guy lives. Chrissakes, I'm a grown man, and I'm still living in my mom's house. Sounds horrible, don't it? And yet I've learned how to be happy under the conditions, and for this I'm grateful. I've certainly got it better than your hypothetical prisoner. What's more, I love my ma. I love taking care of her. It makes me feel worthwhile. It gives me something to do, and what's more she's an interesting person, full of surprises.

Such as?

Do you know she collects Nazi paraphernalia? I take her around to flea markets and estate sales in search of the stuff. It's like a major thing I do for her. She owns a Third Reich flag signed by Joseph Goebbels. Her grandfather, Otto, who fought for Germany in WWI, later became a high-ranking official in the Reich. Oh, and...well I don't have to tell you this. But she also collects all things Elvis.

And so it went, part of the circus that paraded itself as a conversation between Cal and myself.

Cal and I had so many conversations, so many of which were forgettable. I mean the details of the conversations we had were usually eminently forgettable, so we usually found ourselves endlessly repeating ourselves, with small variations. It was always so forgettable what we talked about, but the emotion that I was left with after the conversation, that's what I always seemed to remember, it was like conversation was this thing that two people did. The end of conversation wasn't to arrive at anything, but simply to make the simple music conversation had to offer. Conversation was like being a performer in a musical duet. You spoke back and forth with your instruments, but what was it you really said? Talking with my friends, what few friends I had, we always seemed to loop around in circles, or if not in circles, in long digressive tangents that led you ever further away from where you had started. The end result of such conversations was we never knew what we had accomplished, and we had forgotten what had gotten us going in the first place, but we were always filled with an emotion that we had solved the riddles of the universe.

•

Adeleine was always mystified by my choice in friends. For instance, she always wondered why I spent so much time hanging around with Cal.

I think you've outgrown Cal years ago, haven't you, honey?

It wasn't that Adeleine didn't like Cal—she thought he was a nice enough guy. Harmless, really. She just didn't understand why we spent so much time together.

You're opposites. Don't you see? she liked to point out. He lives a lonely life with his mom, whereas you have a family and your own business.

We're friends from way back, I would point out. No use abandoning ship now.

You're too loyal.

It's loyalty that's kept me with you.

Not love?

Love too, my love. And Cal. He feeds my need to have a friend. That's all. Flawed as he is. I like him. I like our conversations.

Your conversations? What is it you and he sit around and talk about?

This and that.

Is it that personal you can't tell me?

No. I just can't really remember. It's banter really. We banter. Back and forth like a couple of schoolkids.

And that satisfies your need for friendship?

I suppose it does.

Two grown men talking like schoolkids. What does he do all day, anyways?

I don't know.

How could you not know?

I've never asked him.

You've known him all your life and you've never asked him what he does all day at home with his mom?

If he wanted to tell me, I suppose he would. Otherwise I try not to pry. We respect each other's privacy. That's what I like about him. I don't need to explain anything. Just say it and leave it like it is.

I don't understand men, I suppose.

You understand me.

Do I Art? How do you know I understand you?

Now you're getting philosophical.

Well, seriously. I sometimes feel I don't understand you at all.

What don't you understand about me? You get everything there is to get about me. That's why I love you.

Getting you and understanding who you are are two different things, don't you think?

I don't know, are they?

We live with each other, sleep in the same bed night after night, and share many of the same concerns, but there are things about you I still find inscrutable.

Nobody has ever called me inscrutable before.

Sometimes I think you just drift without really having any direction. I don't understand that aspect of you.

What do you mean?

You drift into things, Art. You sometimes don't seem focused. I still don't know why you became a detective. And what's more, I don't think you know why you became a detective. It was an idea you had out of the blue, and then you just pursued it as if it were some great career you were destined for. But as far as I can tell, you don't particularly like the work, and judging from how little money you make from the business, and how much it's costing our family to pay for office rent downtown on Wabash Avenue, and to pay for that woman you hired, it doesn't seem like you're very good at it, either. So yeah...that's what I mean. You drift into things, but you don't seem guided. Your friendship with Cal is another example. You've sustained your friendship to him because, according to you, you have known him so long that there's 'no use jumping ship now.' And yet staying in a friendship just because you have always stayed in a friendship seems a little circular to me. Like drifting.

The same could be said about any relationship that lasts. We stick with it for no other reason than because we always have.

Are you kidding me?

Yes. I'm kidding you.

Another thing...

Yes...

Don't think that I'm not a little irked about how much your business is costing us.

OK. I hear you.

So there is a real price for drifting.

OK. I hear you.

But it's not just the money. I'm irked that you're not doing something more with your life.

I am doing something more.

Of course you're not. Your job as a 'Private Detective' is a joke, and don't think I don't know it.

What brought this on all of a sudden?

I'm just thinking about your laziness. I wish you weren't so lazy.

I'm not lazy. Trust me.

Oh, you're lazy. I love you, but you're lazy. And that's just the beginning of your problems.

Where do they end?

They end—'they' being your problems—they end, ultimately, when you stop being lazy and you start being truthful and you finally figure out who you are.

I am truthful.

Hmmph. I don't know about that. As you say, you're a man who likes his relationships built on routines, but sometimes routines can blind you to the truth of your relationships.

They don't blind me to the truth of our relationship, if that's what you're saying.

They don't? But that's what I am saying. We can have this relationship but you can still be inscrutable to me.

Listen, there's nothing wrong with relationships that are built on routines.

As long as those routines don't blind you to what's really going on.

I'm not blind, if that's what you're saying. I know what's going on.

And then if something comes along and breaks the routine...

Like what?

I don't know. What about that woman you hired for a secretary?

Wanda? What about her?

I don't know what you two do all day locked up in such close quarters.

We work. What do you think we do?

I don't know. But anything can happen, don't you think? If this is a relationship of routine?

It's our marriage.

Our routine is what you said.

It's sacred to me.

But it's still a routine.

Routines can be sacred.

Can they?

They go hand in hand, don't you think?

I always thought the sacred was higher.

It doesn't matter what we think, does it? All that matters is that I love you.

That's a cop out. How do I know you love me, Art?

You're getting too dramatic on me, Adeleine.

Well?

A feeling, I suppose. A gut feeling...

There's no such thing as gut feelings. A gut feeling is what gets you into trouble.

Yeah, but sometimes a gut feeling is all you have to go on. And your gut should tell you by now, my wife, that I love you.

I still don't know how one really knows. You still seems inscrutable to me, Art.

Please. Stop using that word. It scares me.

Well it's true. And if we're going to have conversations like this, then you have to let me speak my mind.

There is truth and then there is truth. Some truths you can think, and you can assume I already know them, but you don't have to say them.

How do I know what you know or don't know?

I think you do know what I know, and I also think I'm not—what's that word?—what do you say I am:

inscrutable? I've never been called that before, and I didn't expect you, of all people, to call me that.

Marriage teaches you that, though. Don't you think? No matter how close you are to somebody, there are still many things you don't know. It's routine that keeps us together, but it's also routine that keeps us from knowing too much of each other. That's what I mean about being truthful.

We know each other's routines. Isn't that the same as knowing somebody? We're only inscrutable when we try to see beyond the routine—as if a person were more than their own odd little collections of routine.

But this doesn't sound like love to me. It sounds like a business partnership: what you and Wanda have. It doesn't sound like what a marriage should be.

What should a marriage be?

Love should be at the root of it, perhaps.

Do you love me?

That's a hard question.

Please don't say it's a hard question. I love you.

How do I know that, Art?

Because I'm telling you it's so. You just have to trust.

Trust...

We have to trust each other.

A business transaction? Is that what this is?

Sort of.

Then I want a new partner. You're not bringing in enough cash.

I never thought the money mattered to you.

That's because I never thought the money mattered to *you*. But apparently it does. And if this is a business partnership, you're not bringing in enough cash.

I'm doing what I can.

You and Wanda.

Wanda is the only thing between my business being viable and my business being doomed.

Wanda. Wanda. Wanda. She does seem too pretty by half.

You're too pretty by half.

You still find me pretty after all these years?

You still care if I find you pretty after all these years?

A woman always cares.

Then I still find you pretty.

Do you find *me* trustworthy, Art?

Yes. Do you find me trustworthy, Adeleine?

The jury's still out.

The jury will always be out.

What can I say? I'm a woman. Women by nature shouldn't trust men.

And vice versa?

Women are trustworthier than men.

Do you think so?

Yes. Women have more to lose.

Well I trust you, even if you don't trust me.

I trust you too, I suppose, though I still think you're a drifter. You have to work on that.

•

She was in the wrong place when she died and she was in the wrong place when we had met.

How had we met? I almost forgot how we met.

Did we meet?

Or had we always known each other?

I feel we have been together so long I don't remember who I was before there was you.

It's the funniest thing, Art. I feel the same way.

Who were you when we met?

I was a girl who lived on the North Shore, and even then I hated being a girl who lived on the North Shore.

What did you hate about it?

I hated everything about it. I lived in a world of princesses and castles and beautiful kingdoms and wealth and prospects and pink dresses and girls who were always so desperate to be the central figure at the ball. But I for one never liked princesses. I've never cared for castles—and I certainly didn't care for what passed for castles on the North Shore. I wanted to find a gypsy to run away with. You were my revolt, Art. You were the thing I was looking for. You were the guy to break me out of my fairy kingdom.

I remember when I met you. You walked through the door to that party and I said: look at the princess.

Yes, and then what?

And then you glared at me like I was the craziest guy you had ever set eyes on.

Because you were the craziest guy I ever set my eyes on.

But I'm not crazy, am I?

You're crazier than most of the guys I have ever known.

How so? How am I crazy?

Do I have to tell you how you're crazy now? We've been together all these years and you don't know how I think you're crazy?

Meg is crazy too, don't you think?

No. I don't think Meg is crazy. I think Meg takes after her mother. She's perfectly sane and rational and like me. She has never liked Princesses.

She liked Dungeons and Dragons.

That was a phase. And what's more, it wasn't about Princesses. She also liked rock and roll.

If you call the Grateful Dead rock and roll.

If it isn't rock and roll what is it?

The Grateful Dead?

And so our conversations went. Round and round in a circle. Who knows what it all meant? What it means. What can it mean when the conversations are remembered, but the sound of the voice isn't remembered? I remember the words, but the sound of her voice. The sound of my wife's voice talking, this I am having the hardest time remembering.

•

Talk to me, Adeleine, talk to me.

Why should I talk to you? You do so well talking to yourself.

I'm not talking to myself. I'm speaking to you.

How can you be speaking to me? I'm no longer here.

But I am still speaking to you. You know that as well as I do.

I suppose so.

I suppose so.

Yes, we suppose so.

•

I was her revolt. And when she was determined to do something, she did it, even if it was revolt. And so, that afternoon early in our relationship—not long after we met and I had mistaken her for a princess—we sat on her parents' sofa. Adeleine seemed so nonchalant about the whole business. I was thrilled to be in the room with her and I felt hyper alive. I couldn't believe my luck.

I hate this house, she said.

Are you crazy? It's a beautiful house!

I hate it. I don't know why. It doesn't seem like home, I suppose.

Are you crazy?

It's a claustrophobic house. She took off a bit of clothes.

I disagree. It's open and airy.

I dislike it. It's too corporate. It's like an office building.

You may dislike it, but to me, coming from where I stand—the bungalow belt—it's a wonderful house. You're lucky to live here.

I'll be lucky to move.

Why don't you show me around? I've never seen a house like this before.

Sure thing, she said, smiling. That I can do.

I didn't think it then, but later when I left her house it occurred to me that I would call Cal and tell him what had happened to me, and he was a guy first and foremost who wouldn't be jealous, and he would listen in disbelief to what happened to me.

I can hear Cal's laughter even now as I recounted the good fortune that had befallen me, running into this woman at a party, and then bumping into her again at the grocery store, and then before I knew it I was getting the complete tour.

Later we would marry—the lavish wedding on the lake. I didn't care for it all: the display of wealth, her parents' country club friends, the snobbery of it all. And frankly, neither did Adeleine, but she recognized it was part of the thing we had to do.

But after the wedding we did what we wanted to, and we drove in a car all the way to a tiny little town,

Chokoloskee, on the Gulf of Mexico near the Everglades in Florida, and we stayed in a shack for fourteen days right on the beach and we didn't do a thing but lay in our bed with the window open to the surf and mosquitoes that we swatted with a fly swatter and at night we would walk on the beach feeling the tug of the tide and the moon and the stars overhead and how they made us feel, not tiny and insignificant, but grateful to be alive even briefly to experience such cosmic grandeur and how many years would go by with us married and intimate and loving.

But the passion of that first day we spent in her parent's house getting to know each other after we first met, while her parents were away—it was a one of a kind experience that started us off on our journey, and she gave it to me, she's the one who made it happen. It was a gift and I'm grateful to her for having given it to me but I'm sad even as I write this that the soulmate I had shared this experience with is no longer with me. I can't turn to her even if I wanted to and say: remember that time at your parents' house when you first brought me home after we ran into each other in the grocery store? In fact, all that was left of that moment was what I could remember of it, and memory was one of those things: maybe you worked it as hard as you could to squeeze all the details out of it, but the problem with memory as far as I could see was you could never quite be sure if what you remembered really happened. Memory was like standing on the sand in the surf. Here you are with your feet planted firmly in the sand, and yet as the cool bubbly surf rolls in you feel the sand erode under your feet and what seemed like terra firma is suddenly less firma and less terra too for that matter.

Oh, memory! What part of you is real and what part imagined, and even real or imagined, who else could possibly care what occurred in the privacy of her parents' bedroom that afternoon so many years ago? For even if I said, this is what happened, exactly as I describe it, is there a soul in this busy hectic world who would care? Meg maybe, a little, but no kid really wants the details of that, and after that it matters less to each generation, so who would even care?

·

I lay in bed in the hotel room with Rita and I couldn't decide whether to retain the memory I had had of that afternoon with Adeleine or to banish it from my memory forever.

Like Adeleine, Rita too had removed her clothes, and we tried to have sex, but it didn't work so well. I couldn't escape the sense of déjà vu, not to mention I was older now, so much water under the bridge this time, and when she seemed miffed after a few minutes of her effort failed to register on me she looked up and spoke.

What's the problem?

Should I tell her I'm an old man? Old and broken?

There is no problem.

This is a problem.

This is life, I told her.

It's not a very friendly life. I thought you liked me.

I do like you.

I mean I thought you found me attractive.

I do find you attractive.

Then what's this?

The tone of Rita's response after that first time established forever the tone of our relationship. It didn't take any time at all, I tell myself now, to go from hellos to hell. And once I was in hell I haven't been able to figure out a way to escape.

•

It was the first time but not the last time I had had a problem with Rita. I hated having problems in bed with Rita but I knew what my problem was. I had never had such problems with Adeleine.

But of course I couldn't say that. All I could say was: I'm sorry Rita. I don't mean to have problems.

OK, then. Let's not have any problems.

I'll try.

And try I did, but I still had problems.

Is it me? she asked.

Of course it isn't, I said, which was true and not true.

I don't like the way you said that.

What do you mean?

You weren't convincing. Maybe it is me that's the problem.

She got up from bed and started putting her clothes on.

No. Come back to bed. You're not the problem.

Then what's the problem?

There is no problem.

She took off her clothes and came back to bed.

OK, let's try this again.

So we tried it again, but I had a problem.

You're still having a problem.

I hate to have this problem. I don't know how to explain it.

It's me.

No it's not.

Yes it is. If it were someone you were attracted to, you wouldn't be having this problem.

The problem is I cannot believe my wife is dead. I think this without saying it: the problem is I cannot believe my wife is dead. Her death is like smelling salts in my nose. I can't get the strong sensation of those smelling salts out of my nose. The problem is: How do I tell Rita that my problem is related to my dead wife? Is this how I say it? I'm having a problem because I cannot believe my wife is dead.

I didn't know how to say it.

I thought of opening a bottle of champagne. I thought maybe that would help. I told Rita that's what I was going to do. I had a bottle chilling in my office across the street.

Do you want me to come with?

No, just stay here. Watch a movie or something. I'll be right back.

But you're coming back, right, Art?

Right.

Promise?

Promise.

You wouldn't skip out on me, Art, would you?

No.

Not over this? I can live with this.

Baby I'm going out to get champagne so we can fix this. Or if not fix it, just sit and have a little champagne. I'll be back. Promise.

Thank you, Art. Seriously. I thank you.

It's good we found each other.

Yes.

OK. Bye.

Bye.

I'll see you in fifteen minutes.

Fifteen. I'm counting the minutes.

So long...

I took the elevator down. The lobby of the hotel was packed with business people just in from meetings at a convention. They were making dinner plans. Outside the hotel, cabs cruised the streets like sharks. I crossed the street and went up the elevator to my office on the fifteenth floor. This was where I had found her, three months before. Before that, my office had meant other things, but now it will always mean that, in addition to those things.

•

I found her in my office, on the floor. She wasn't supposed to be there, but she was there. There wasn't a part of her body that was spared a bullet.

I don't want to tell you where she was shot but her body, from her head down to her feet, was riddled with bullet holes. He shot her hands—was she blocking herself with them, and he shot right through them? He shot her feet—why her feet? Did he tell her dance, and take aim at them? He shot her in her private parts and he hit her belly and he unloaded several shots into her side and into her core—the bullets breaking ribs, shredding the spine, shattering femur and shin bone and shoulder blade. There was a graze wound to her throat and a point-blank shot to her forehead...two more shots to her face...a missing eyeball...

There wasn't a place on her body—my wife's body—without an entry or an exit wound. Bullets ricocheting all over the place through her body...

And my hand...I touched every one of those holes: soft, the heat mostly disappeared from her body, the sticky blood coagulating. I touched gingerly, unable to believe what I touched, unable to get my mind to slip forward into a comprehension of what had happened, unable, practically, to move—except for my finger, which traced a slow circle around each of her wounds.

When the police came, they asked me to step aside. Get outside the perimeter, they said. One of the police actually pushed me so I almost stumbled backwards. Step outside the perimeter. He was wearing blue surgical gloves.

Another officer stood next to me. He said something into his radio mouthpiece, which was firmly attached to a strap on his torso. He said: Victim. Female. 42 years old. Gunshot wound to temple. Gunshot wound to forehead. Two gunshot wounds to face. Gunshot wound to neck. Three gunshot wounds to abdomen. Two gunshot wounds to pelvis. One gunshot wound to kidney. Gunshot wounds to both hands—left and right. Gunshot wounds to legs—shattering femurs. Gunshot wounds to left foot and to right foot. Seventeen 9mm casings at site of shooting.

He turned and asked me:

Who was the dead body?

I told him it was Adeleine Topp.

Did you know the dead body?

She was my wife.

Did you touch or disturb the dead body?

Yes. I touched her wounds. I fell on her.

Did anyone else touch or disturb the dead body when the dead body fell?

No.

As far as you know, did anyone else touch or observe the dead body when the dead body fell?

No.

Was the dead body dead when the dead body fell?

I don't know.

And on the questions went, and so too the investigation into her death, until it all stopped, and then I found myself alone and wandering.

•

I crossed the street and went up the elevator to my office on the fifteenth floor and said: Good afternoon, Wanda.

Hello, Art.

How goes it?

She was bent over a crossword puzzle.

Where've you been? Out searching for business?

Sort of...

Any luck?

Sort of.

How 'bout here, Wanda? Any calls I need to be made aware of?

Finnegan's Wake wife?

What?

The crossword puzzle. Three down. *Finnegan's Wake* wife?

Who's Finnegan?

That's what I want to know.

Sounds like an Irishman.

Fin. Finnegan. Think of an Irish name for a woman.

Mary?

Mary. I'll try Mary.

Any calls?

Cal called.

What did he want?

He didn't say.

Any others?

Three calls. All wrong numbers. I really think we ought to change the number around here. We keep getting confused with Triple AAA Plumbing.

I should have been a plumber.

Well, you'd certainly get more calls if you had been.

If I had been...had been.

Where are the champagne glasses?

There—on the shelf in the closet where you keep your extra clothes.

I met this woman...

Oh, Art! I'm so happy you're moving on!

Not moving on yet.

But a woman? Who is she?

I don't know really. Some lady I met at the...Get this, I met her at the cemetery.

Better to meet someone at the cemetery, Art, than at the...

At the what?

Oh, Art...I'm just so happy you're getting out and meeting people.

I was putting flowers on my wife's grave is all. And then this woman...

Is she pretty Art?

I don't know, Wanda. I've forgotten what pretty is. I've been in love too long with my wife to know pretty.

You've never been in love too long to know pretty.

You're pretty, Wanda.

Thank you, Art. But be careful what you say. It can get you into trouble. Harassment.

Are you going to sue me now, Wanda?

No. Not you Art. You're too nice to sue—though I might get you in trouble for all the useless clues you give me on my crossword puzzle.

I said Mary.

It's not Mary.

Where are the champagne glasses?

What do you want those for?

She's in the hotel waiting for me.

She...

This woman I met in the cemetery.

What's her name?

I don't have time to talk about her now. She's waiting for me in the hotel room. At least I think she's waiting for me. She may be gone by now.

She's waiting for you in the hotel room? Art, what did you go and get a hotel room for?

I don't know, Wanda. I met her at the cemetery and we had lunch at Giovanni's, and before I knew it one thing led to another.

Were you drinking?

We had a few.

A what?

We had some wine.

Oh, Art...

She's in grieving mode too. Grief. We both are. She wears a veil.

Her husband?

No, her mom.

What about her husband?

Her husband—I don't know that she has a husband.

Can you think of a word for 'handy' that starts with a 'k'?

No. Can you?

It's five letters.

I can't think. Where are the glasses?

Over there, Art, on the shelf in the closet where you keep your clothes, like I said.

Sorry Wanda. I'm a bit confused today.

I imagine so.

Thanks for being here.

It's my job to be here.

No it isn't. Or yes it is. But thank you all the same. I'm going to be going.

What's her name, Art? You must remember her name. That's so important for a woman—to remember her name.

Thanks for asking. As a matter of fact I almost forgot.

What is it?

It's a four-letter word that starts with R.

Rena?

No. Close.

Give me a clue.

Sounds like pita.

Such a lovely name. Rita. Is she pretty?

I'll tell you tomorrow.

Do you want me to lock up when I leave?

Yes. Lock up. And krafty.

What?

Crafty with a 'k.' Those handymen are always spelling things with Ks. For your krossword.

Crafty has six letters.

Oh.

Goodnight Art.

Goodnight Wanda.

Good luck to you.

And to you.

•

I took the elevator down to the lobby of my building. The bellman was nowhere to be seen. He was thought to be having an affair with a woman on the thirteenth floor. We were all thought to be having affairs, I thought, as I walked out of there. I'm having an affair, I thought. I'm having an affair behind my wife's back. This isn't right.

And then I heard my wife.

It is right, Art.

No it's not, Adeleine.

Honey, I'm dead. No use in worrying about me anymore. Go on and live your life.

I don't want to live it without you, Adeleine.

Oh Art. That's such a funny thing to say.

It's not meant to be funny. It's the truth.

What about Meg? She needs you.

Meg doesn't need me, Adeleine, and you know that. Meg hasn't needed me in years. And now with you gone, she needs me even less than ever.

You're not doing enough to reach out to her.

What am I supposed to do? She doesn't return my phone calls. I send her letters and never receive a response in return. For all I know she never returned to Tulane. She may be working in California for all I know.

Art, you worry too much. I'm dead. There's no need to think of me anymore. Move on with your life. Be happy. You only have one life to live. You don't know how long you have left. You may live to old age like I always thought you would, or you may die tomorrow.

I would like that. I can't take you not being here.

But look what you have in your hands.

What do I have?

You have two champagne glasses and a bottle of champagne.

Do you want to sit down and have champagne with me?

No. I don't want to have champagne with anyone anymore. Not after what happened.

Oh, Adeleine. About what happened...

No use worrying about it now, Art. What's done is done.

What was done? Did you suffer?

I suffered. Yes. That I can say. I suffered. More than words can say. But it's over now.

Don't tell me you suffered. Please don't tell me you suffered. I can't take it that you suffered.

But it's over now, Art, and it's time for you to move on.

It's not time for me to move on. Quit saying that. I want to be with you.

No, go find that woman. Drink your champagne while it's still cold, while there's still dew on the bottle.

Our bed is still warm. I swear I feel you at night when I fall to sleep.

I'm gone, Art. There's no reason to hold on. Go find your lady friend. Where did you meet her, by the way?

You know where I met her.

No I don't.

Of course you do.

No, seriously.

No, seriously!

Art, please. Your champagne...she's waiting.

I'll go under one condition.

Say the word, darling.

Under the condition you're never far from me.

I'll never be far from you, Art. Now go and enjoy your life. Seriously. Listen to me. Don't be foolish.

•

I crossed traffic and was nearly run down. I couldn't keep my directions straight. I looked right when I should have looked left. I was confused all of a sudden. Out of sorts. I tried to get back to Rita as soon as possible, before the bottle of champagne cooled.

And the intimacy didn't feel intimate. In fact, I felt exposed laying with her...exposed. I didn't know how to escape...

And then I was trembling. Trembling while she tried to calm me. I found I suffered bouts of terror. Post-traumatic stress syndrome. And this talking of hurt and brokenness was more than I could take.

I awoke in the middle of the night, still in my clothes while she slept the sleep of the dead next to me.

In the morning she was gone, and there was a note: *Call me, R.*

PART II: JUST SHOOT ME

The interview should have been innocuous. I don't recall anything about the situation that seemed abnormal. A man and a woman were getting divorced. I was hired by the wife's lawyer to interview the husband. His name was Adolph Meyer. At the time, it meant nothing to me.

•

That was then. This is now. Since Adeleine died, the adventure of my life has worn thin.

Maybe it's the detective business and all the disappointments that have made me surly. I don't know. Maybe it's everything combined.

I feel at heart as if I'm a nice person but I also know that I don't come off that way, not since Adeleine died.

A lot of people find me difficult to get along with. Just look at Rita. We've spent five years together, on and off, and we've been at an impasse the last year or so. She feels I'm too crabby. I'm always down in the dumps. She doesn't like the attitude.

I tell her—I say: There are facts and attitudes, Rita. If you don't like my attitude, change the fact.

Don't worry, buster, I might, she keeps threatening.

I keep making pledges to be nice to her. I try to be friendly when I see her. I always make a point of keeping a smile on my face when I talk to her, but she's not convinced.

You're not happy, she tells me.

Yes I am.

No you're not.

Yes I am, I tell her. Just look at the smile on my face.

You may have a smile on your face, but there's a tone in your voice and I don't like it. It's irascible.

What do you mean? Irascible?

You know what I mean.

No I don't.

Yes you do.

No.

Yes.

And we go back and forth like this until not only is the tone in my voice irascible but whatever smile I had plastered to my face is gone and I'm shouting at her with genuine rage and anger.

Maybe this thing with Rita isn't meant to be. I've never fought with a woman so much my entire life. Adeleine and I never fought.

I once told Rita this in the heat of an argument.

What is it with you? I asked her.

With me?

Yeah. You're always causing arguments. It seems like all we do is fight.

You're the one who does all the fighting, Art. I want nothing to do with fighting.

Then stop starting them.

It's you, Art, who starts them.

It is not.

Yes it is.

Listen, I tell her. Before I met you I never had an argument my whole life. Adeleine and I were married for eighteen years and we never had a single fight that I can think of.

That's because you're idealizing her, Art. Don't you see this?

I am not idealizing her. I wish she were here right now to support me on this issue. We never had a fight.

Yeah right, Rita says. If you're so holy, how come you don't talk to your daughter anymore? If you're so high and mighty, why has your daughter estranged you?

It was the accident that estranged me and my daughter.

Then it's the accident that has made you irascible.

It is not.

It is too.

And so we'd go back and forth until finally I'd storm out of her apartment and live on my own for a few days. Do laundry, collect mail, pay bills. Stuff like that.

Fact is, maybe Rita's right. Maybe I don't present as nice a mug to the world as I think I do. I seem to recall making a point of being nice, especially while I worked in the telecom industry. But a lot of good that did me. Then the HR personnel took me out. After that, I was less inclined to be nice. Then Adeleine died and it's only gotten worse. I get surly with the gas station clerk for no reason. I honk my horn at poor drivers and pedestrians that get in the way. The other day I blew my horn at a lady pushing her baby stroller. She was pushing the stroller through the intersection while talking on her phone. She didn't seem to be in any hurry getting through the intersection.

I told her to go fuck herself and her baby too, and I flipped her the bird as I sped by.

Now I see it wasn't such a nice thing to say. I regret having said it. I don't wish any misfortune upon that woman or her baby. Having lived through some misfortune myself, I wouldn't wish hurt upon anyone in the world.

•

Now you're feeling sorry for yourself.

No I'm not.

Yes you are.

Blurt. Blurt.

Pop. Pop. Pop.

•

I never told Adeleine this, but I never used a gun in my job. I suppose that made me just as righteous as that stripper and her bouncer, but Adeleine made such a fuss over this aspect of the job that I decided it would be better to try and do business without one. I soon learned that best practice was not to carry a gun or any type of official ID. It was better to blend in and be as normal as possible. What's more, the sorts of cases I did were all small potato cases. Nothing very interesting. I most often worked in conjunction with a couple of divorce lawyers—they'd send me off to ask questions of people. My job, more often than not, was to establish an informal back-channel line of conversation to find out what was negotiable and what was not negotiable.

In some cases, the legal warfare between divorcing spouses would escalate so rapidly that I was called to try and defuse the tension. I'd often meet one or the other or both of the competing spouses and I'd try and help them see things in a more reasonable light. Again, my goal was to try and defuse tension, particularly in an escalating conflict. I always tried to meet the husband or the wife in a neutral and calming public place. I'd meet these people, and I'd try and use the only tool I really had, the gift of gab. I had a long-standing conviction that a reasonable solution could always be arrived at through talk, and as a result that expensive litigation could be avoided.

Sometimes I was successful at this sort of thing. Folks naturally found me to be approachable and reasonable. I had empathy for everyone I dealt with. I assume that everyone, except in very rare cases, is at heart a good actor. Let's face it, no one really wants to have to confront divorce head-on, especially when children are involved. So in my conversations I would point to ways around the stress, the turmoil, and in many cases the heartbreaking tragedy of volatile divorce proceedings. Let's everyone try and be reasonable here. If we're reasonable now, we all can get on with our lives. In divorce there will inevitably be harm and foul, but of course the shrapnel that comes from divorce can maim everyone, including the kids. A little effort working behind the scenes can reduce that shrapnel, so let's talk it out. Let's talk about a pathway that makes sense for everyone, including you...

I was naturally pretty good at this type of work. My method was to wing it. I was always winging it. I felt I was always talking off the cuff and hoping for the best. Occasionally I tried to imagine that I was on the receiving end of a divorce proceeding, and how painful that would be for me. It was this thinking that guided me in conversations with estranged spouses. I tried to be gentle as a lamb with them, and respectful. To me, they had just found themselves on the wrong side of luck. For one reason or another, love, which had maybe once sprung true and beautiful, had turned south on them. I understood the hurt, the anger. And maybe this is why I kept getting called to participate in these sorts of cases. But these cases never paid much, and there weren't enough of them to build a sustainable business on. At the end of the day, a lot of people preferred all-out warfare in divorce proceedings, shrapnel and children be damned.

•

Adolph Meyer and I got together for the interview in a neutral place—a café of his choice on the north side—and I asked him a few questions about what was prompting the divorce. He claimed he didn't want the divorce. It was his wife who insisted on getting divorced. He was happy in love with her.

I asked him several standard questions: Did you have any affairs? Did you sign a prenup agreement? Are you going to seek custody of the children?

After a while of asking questions, he told me point blank: What you don't seem to understand...

Hold on, I told him. I turned on my recorder and got out a pen and paper.

What you don't seem to understand, detective...

Yes. Go ahead.

Is that it's guys like you who are ruining this country.

Oh yes? How so?

Guys like you. Leeches. You feed off of the misery of others. You make your living off guys like me.

I'm a detective, I pointed out. I'm a neutral party.

You're not neutral. You feed off of others' misfortune. Do you know, if this marriage of mine falls apart, I'm done for. I can't bear the thought of losing my wife.

If your marriage falls apart it is the fault of you and your wife.

You're dead wrong there, detective. It's the fault of leeches like you and that dirty lawyer of hers. What's her lawyer doing getting involved in a case like this? Money. It's all greed. My wife and I, we have a perfectly normal relationship. But the lawyer doesn't care. You and the lawyer are only interested in one outcome.

Sir, I pointed out. I'm only doing my job. I have nothing against you or your wife. I don't know who either of you are. I don't even know the case.

The case is, he interrupted. The case is my wife is seeking to divorce me for no reason whatsoever.

Surely there's a reason.

There is no reason, detective. She's unhappy, is all. Is being unhappy grounds for a divorce? 'Til death do us part...that was the agreement she signed on for. We have five kids. You don't divorce your husband because you're unhappy.

Then there must be some other cause. Do you care to speculate?

I'll speculate. She's going through menopause. That's all it is. She's having a down time. She's depressed. She's unhappy. Her hair is turning gray and she's got a wrinkle. She's turning into an old lady and she doesn't like it. She's blaming her troubles on me. That's all. It's not me who's caused her to be unhappy. It's a biological condition called old age. But I have five kids and I can't *emotionally* afford to be separated from them. I had six and lost one to leukemia two years ago. He was only eight years old. My youngest. After he died, my wife started to have her menopause. With that came her depression, for which she blames me. Do you have any idea, detective, what it is like to live with someone who is chronically depressed?

No.

Always being blamed for one thing or another is what it's like. From morning 'til night, the screaming that takes place in my house. The screaming that comes from her mouth. The screaming and screaming about how it's my fault everything has gone to hell. What do you mean? I ask my wife. What's going to hell? You know what's gone to hell, she tells me. Everything has gone to hell. This family has gone to hell. Our relationship has gone to hell. There is no more happiness in our family. I need oxygen, she keeps telling me. I need a breath of fresh air. I can't take it anymore. I need for you to move on. That's what she keeps telling me, how she feels trapped. She tells me I need to move on because she's unhappy. But the way I see it, being unhappy isn't grounds for a divorce. We sign on for life. That's what marriage is. It's a life-long commitment. 'Til death do us part. A divorce…let me be frank with you, detective. A divorce would kill me. It would utterly destroy me. I know you see me here ranting and raving and you think I'm a madman. I can tell by the way you're looking at me. I can tell you think I'm a lunatic. You're trying to hide your judgment of me, but I see your smirk. I can see the smirk on your face. Please. Remove the smirk.

No sir. With all due respect, I am far from smirking.

I am not a madman, I tell you. I'm a reasonable man who's angry. I'm angry that my wife's menopause is threatening me. I'm pissed off that you and a dirty lawyer are trying to do me in. This is what makes me angry. Not angry. Berserk with anger. I'm berserk. This whole thing is making me berserk. I can't believe it's happening to me. I'm a normal man whose wife has gotten out of control and now she, you, and a lawyer are threatening to destroy me.

With all due respect, sir, this isn't about destroying you.

I have five living kids that depend on me, detective. I don't need people like you and that high-priced scumbag lawyer of hers to try and take it away from me.

I'm recording all this, I hope you know…

You're smirking is what you're doing. You're smirking at me, and if you don't remove the smirk from your face you will pay a high price, I promise you, detective.

I'm not smirking.

You sit there and you think you're safe. You laugh at me. You think I'm some kind of monkey. The truth is I have dedicated myself for twenty-eight years to this family of mine, and I don't intend for anyone to take it away from me. I'm a bricklayer. Do you know what that is? A bricklayer is a slave. Someone who gets his balls busted every hour of the day and who comes home dead tired from work. A bricklayer is someone who actually works for a living. Do you even know what work is, detective? I will tell you what work is. It's not sitting in coffee shops like this trying to ruin people's lives. I stand on a scaffold all day with a trowel in hand laying bricks. Or in my case, heavy blocks. All day long laying sixty-pound blocks. Day after day. Week after week. Year after year. I lay them in hundred-degree weather while you sit in your air-conditioned office. My skin scorched by the sun. I lay them in the winter, too. My fingers so cold I can hardly pick the blocks up. The antifreeze they put in the mortar to keep it from freezing destroys my skin. I work my ass off building buildings while guys like you sit around interviewing people in coffee shops. I don't have time like you to sit around in coffee shops sipping coffee, detective. I can't afford to miss a day of work. Unlike you, if I miss a day of work my family goes hungry. Do you think I would have been able to carry on with this labor all these years if I knew that it was only going to result in my wife taking it all away from me? Taking it away because she became unhappy because she noticed a wrinkle in her skin? Do you think that a man like me is going to let an unhappy woman and a money-hungry lawyer and a fucked-up detective who's never worked a day in his life take away from me the only thing in this world that I have? My family?

Sir, if you want, we can end this interview right now.

I will tell you this, detective. This ain't no game. You want to spy on me and break up my marriage? You want to try and ruin my life? Well I can play that game too. Believe me.

Sir, it's your wife who started all of this. Without her initiating this, neither the lawyer nor myself would be here.

You fuel the fire is what you do, detective. You fan the flames. If you think you can win this, you are sorely mistaken. I am stronger than you, and I know how to play this game too, if I want to.

Sir, with all due respect, as I mentioned, I am recording this conversation. You do realize that...

Too late for that. Too late for anything.

Is there anything else you need to tell me, sir? Because I am afraid I won't be able to continue under the conditions...

Under the conditions, you would do well to leave me alone. That's all I have to say.

OK, then, this interview is done.

I stopped the recorder.

Have a nice day, I told him.

He pushed the table so it cut into my gut, and tilting his head said: You already crossed the line. I'm on to you, detective.

Abruptly, he was gone.

I watched him disappear down the sidewalk. He had a loping stride. His arms seemed powerful, dangerous. He wore work boots coated in dried concrete. I tried to imagine what he would do to me. Beat me over the head with those hands of his? A red bandana hung from his rear pocket and swung in cadence to his walk. He turned left around the corner and was gone out of my life.

•

I called Cal. What are you doing?

I'm lifting weights and pluming pot smoke out my window. I'm still paranoid my mom is going to catch me smoking weed.

Cal, you're a grown man. Are you telling me she doesn't know you smoke weed?

I never told her.

Surely she can smell it on you, don't you think? After all these years?

I've never been certain what my mom can smell or not. I'm not sure her nose is very good. If she were a bird dog, we'd have to retire her. Thankfully, she's just a fluffy old poodle with bad joints. Now what do you want Art? You caught me between reps. I'm trying to build up my pecs.

Your pecs?

Yeah. Right now, they're too loose and flabby. Like a girl's breasts. I want to get rid of them. I've been bench pressing.

You and I used to bench press, if I remember...

At Steinmetz. That's how we met, big guy. You always had the muscle and the brains, Art. That's why I stuck with you.

The question is, Cal, why have I stuck with you?

Because you're a loyal son of a bitch? I don't know. Because I showed you how to fire a gun and not kill yourself in the process?

Speaking of which, Cal, are you available to go shooting? I just finished up an interview and I'm at loose ends. I wouldn't mind firing off a few rounds to release stress.

An interview. Look at you go.

It's what I do. It's my job.

Yeah, Art, but I never hear you talk about your work. Sometimes I wonder if you really do run your own business.

It's just business is slow. Nothing more than that. How about I be over in a half hour?

How 'bout I just pick you up instead, Art?

How about?

I'll meet you at your office in fifteen.

Sounds like a plan.

•

There were a bunch of people in front of my building on Wabash: office workers, commuters, smokers. I pushed through and took the elevator up.

I deposited the recorder in a safe I kept in my desk.

Wanda was playing solitaire on the computer.

How'd it go, Art?

How'd what go?

The interview, is what.

Which interview are you talking about?

The only one you've had the past three weeks. The one with the bricklayer.

We met at a coffee shop. I interviewed him.

And...

He certainly doesn't want to break up with his wife.

When she came in here it was sure as hell clear she wanted to break up with him.

It doesn't work so well if the break-up is coming from one side and not both.

No. I don't suppose it ever does.

Speaking of marriages, how's Ed?

He's wonderful, Art. Thank you for asking. He's taking me to the opera tonight. That's why I'm playing solitaire.

I don't get it. What's the connection?

It empties my brain. I like to have a clear mind before the opera.

When I stepped outside, the commuters were still thick in front of the building. A moment later, Cal pulled up doing fifty miles an hour and came to a screeching halt sending gravel and bits of debris from the curb flying against my shins. Folks at the edge of the sidewalk reflexively leaped back.

Hurry up! Get in, Art! He banged the horn like something important was about to happen.

I hopped into the car and off he went, screeching the tires as he pulled out.

What's the rush? The faces of the crowd were blurred for a second in the windshield glass.

No rush, Art! No rush at all! Who's in a rush? I'm just antsy sitting all day nothing to do! It drives me nuts!

•

At the range, he fired his Uzi. *BLURT. BLURT.* When he was done, I stood ready and fired my gun.

Pop. Pop. Pop.

One thing, he said, placing his hand on my shoulder. He was wearing earplugs. I was wearing muffs, so he had to shout.

What?

One thing, Art...

What's that? I asked. I fired six more shots into the target and was disappointed to see my accuracy was for shit.

I never liked that Ruger. It's old and it doesn't shoot well. I'm surprised you're so attached to it.

It's not attachment.

Then why don't you upgrade, Art?

Because I bought a shitload of Federal high-velocity 40 grain ammo. A bulk purchase. It was a fire sale, and I paid for it with a one-time-only cash bonus I got back when times were flush in telecom. Until it's gone, this is the only gun I'm gonna shoot.

I fired off a few more rounds.

Are you going for the nuts? Or is that just bad shooting?

Do I have to answer that?

Try hitting the target instead.

I loaded up and gave it another go.

Pathetic, Cal said. No wonder all you do is divorce cases. If you actually knew how to shoot a gun...if you actually had a real gun to shoot, maybe you'd do better in life.

You think?

I know. In fact...

Cal disappeared a moment. When he came back, he handed me a gun case.

Try this on for size. It might work better for you. It's a Glock 26 semi-automatic with the seventeen-round magazine. See how it fits.

He opened the case and handed me the gun. The gun was a matte black Glock with a rubberized handle.

Go ahead, Art, try it on for size. I'm tired of watching you shoot that rusted .22. It makes no sense.

I don't want your gun, Cal.

I bought that gun two years ago down at a gun show in Hollywood, Florida, and I keep it in my glove compartment for safety purposes. But it ain't doing me no good in my glove compartment. I've been meaning to give it to you because I don't like that Ruger. But now in your job you can actually use it. Take it, you're a friend. I feel responsible for you. Also, with a gun like this, who knows? You might actually move up in the world as a detective.

Move up? I shook my head.

Nobody is gonna ever take you seriously if they see you carrying a .22. Don't you want to do something interesting in your business other than divorce cases?

My business is interesting enough. Besides I got all this ammo.

That's a lame excuse, Art. Just try the gun, for fuck's sake!

I stepped into the lane and worked a round into the chamber and I started firing just like that. *Pow. Pow. Pow. Pow. Pow.* Immediately, I felt adrenalized.

Excellent shooting Art! You're actually hitting the target. Try again.

I took aim and shot. *Pow. Pow. Pow.*

Nice shooting, Art. That's the best I've ever seen you do. How's it feel?

I don't know. It's a good looking gun. I'm not used to firing something so beautiful.

It is a beautiful piece, cowboy!

Now you're starting to sound like John Wayne.

You make me want to sound like John Wayne. Now shoot, cowboy!

I closed my eyes and pulled the trigger in rapid succession and I couldn't believe what a remarkable gun it was. Hail Mary full of grace, I said, and fired off the rest of the rounds in the clip. Cal had another clip loaded and he handed it to me. Have at it, big guy.

I started shooting again, and he was there behind my shoulder, sighting along with me.

You got much better control with this gun than you have with that Ruger.

Yes, I agree, I told him. I kept shooting.

I am slightly concerned that it's too small in those big fucking hands of yours. I might have to get the gun adjusted for you.

It's fine. No need to worry.

Also, how does it sight?

Well I seem able to hit the target, so I guess it sights just fine. *Pow. Pow. Pow. Pow. Pow. Pow.*

Hole in one, Cal said, when we drew the target up to see my tight pattern. Excellent job, my friend. So it ain't your skill that's been the problem, it's that fucking Ruger.

Or maybe I'm just lucky today.

How do you like the gun?

It's a beautiful gun, Cal. Thanks for letting me shoot it.

Keep it, he said. It's yours. I have a few magazines for you and three boxes of ammo. Keep it in your office. In your job I don't like to see you fucking around with a pussy gun.

No thanks, Cal.

Yes thanks. Take it, pally, and don't fuck with me.

Can I pay you for it?

Yeah, pay me by using it! Pay me by getting rid of that shitty Ruger.

Well then thank you, Cal, I said.

When I was done, Cal stepped to the lane with his Uzi and shot at the target without discrimination, tearing it up, the gun going *BLURT! BLURT! BLURT! BLURT! BLURT!* The shell casings flew out of the gun and littered the floor; the tattered paper target danced on the clips, then fell like confetti. When he was done he gave a little chuckle like he was proud of himself.

Man! That cleaned my clock like smelling salts! All day long pent up in my house wasting time. I thought I was going to go crazy, Art.

He reloaded a clip, dropped one in the chamber, and let loose. Wham. Bam. Thank you ma'am! *BLURT. BLURT. BLURT!* Then he unloaded again...Wango zee tango! Wango, tango! Blam! Blam! Blam! *BLURT. BLURT. BLURT!* And again. *BLURT. BLURT. BLURT!*

When it's all over he removed his earplugs and he was as happy as a clam.

You're as happy as a clam, aren't you!

I sure am! And you know what I like about clams?

No I don't.

The soft slippery interior.

I chuckled and shook my head and said: You're a funny guy, Cal!

•

After shooting we had a couple beers and he told me about his life.

How are you getting along, buddy? I asked. It's a question I never asked. In fact, I didn't know much about the guy.

Wonderfully, he said. I couldn't be happier. I live in a small house with my aging mother. Did I tell you I started to go to church again?

Again? I didn't know you ever went to church.

I used to go religiously. My father was a great believer in the Church. He held the coin basket. Hell, I was even an altar boy for a few years. Let me tell you. The church I went to. In the winter it was freezing, in the summer it was hotter than hell. It was a crazy place to be an altar boy. Anyways I started going again.

Why?

I don't know exactly. Though a month or two ago I found in the bottom of my underwear drawer this cross someone gave me for my First Communion. I was cleaning, believe it or not, and I found it there in the back of the drawer. I used to wear that cross all the time during my pimply years. Then the little washer that held the cross to the neck chain got loose, and the cross kept falling off. I used to love that cross. Here, I carry it in my pocket now. Let me show you.

He handed me the cross.

The thing I like about it is what it says on the back.

I flipped it over to look.

There...that expression: "I am a Catholic. In case of an accident, please call a priest." When I saw it again it really got to me. There was something there that I responded to all of a sudden.

Like what? I handed the cross back to him and tilted my beer bottle. Cheers.

God bless.

It's only a phrase.

Yes, but the way it says it: I am a Catholic. Art, you know as well as I do, all my life I have drifted. I have never felt like I belonged to anything. Ask me what I am or who I am and all I could tell you was my name. For the most part that's all I have. I've been in and out of so many jobs I can't even tell you for certain what I do for a living or what my so-called expertise is. And now that I've been out of work so long, I don't know what to tell others it is I do. When I go for job interviews I don't know how to put myself all together so that the identity of a single person emerges from the picture. I've been on this earth too long to have such a vague resume. Most people after they have lived as long as I have can define themselves. Say what they do. Me, I can't. At heart I take care of my mom. She's the personality in my family. She's the one with all the friends. She plays bingo like crazy and card games with all of her lady friends—they come over to the house. She entertains them, and I make sure everything is OK. I make sure we don't run out of tea or cookies or cake, and the thermostat is set just right, and that we have a little brandy for later in the night. But my mother is in the center of it all. She's laughing. She's telling stories of my father. She tells stories of me. I can tell she's still proud of me, but I feel I've let her down. But she's got her place in the world. Me, my place in the world has so far been to look after her. And to look after you, I suppose.

Me?

You, Art. You're my only friend in the whole goddamned world.

Oh, come on.

No, serious. So when I saw that cross again with the expression, "I am a Catholic," well, by God, I thought...I suppose I am. After all, I was raised Catholic. I was confirmed. I know the prayers. I've done confession. It's something I can claim for myself and try to be. And so I've been going to church to see what it's like being a Catholic. I think it's who I am.

But do you believe in that Jesus shit?

I don't know that I do. But I believe in the Church. I believe in kneeling in the pews. I believe in the light that filters through the stained-glass windows. And by the way, I volunteered to take the collection basket around, and now I'm doing that, just like my dad did. It's a good feeling. I feel better about myself.

Good. I'm glad.

It beats everything else I do.

Like what?

Like when my mother's not around, I watch porn. I'm tired of porn. Do you have any idea how much porn I watch? I don't understand it. I don't understand why I watch it so much. It's not like I like it. It's alien to me. I don't understand the people in it. It's pussy and cock. It's not even people. Just items. I've watched too much of it. I'm worried it's soured me and made me useless for the real thing. I don't want two-dimensional pussy, and the jack that everlastingly screws it. What I want is the thing that goes with the pussy. I want the woman. The real thing: the person. Hell, I don't even give a damn about pussy, when you come right down to it. When you come right down to it, I'd be content just to hold hands with a woman who cared to listen to me and smile with me at the sunset.

A romantic...

A romantic, yes, and there's nothing wrong with that, Art.

I agree.

I'm hoping going to church again will help me clear up some of these issues. I already feel like I'm cutting down on my porn. I went to confession and told the priest about it, and I've been two weeks now without it.

Wow, good.

I'm hoping that by going to church I may even meet a woman. It's a long shot, but it's just one of my thoughts.

Here's hoping.

All my life, I've been looking for women at bars or the racetrack. Or even the shooting range. Remember that crazy woman I took home from the shooting range who wanted to 'play' that I was killing her? The one that had me bind and gag her and shoot blanks at her?

She left you too.

Yes, thank God. But not before extracting several hundred dollars from me. But I was glad to get rid of her. I would have paid much more than that to see her go. Anyways, these are all the wrong places to find a woman. You want a drunk? Go looking for her in the bar. You want a gambling addict? You'll find her at the horse track. You want a freak? You'll meet one at the gun club. But if you want a wife, well maybe the place to look is at church.

Then you just end up with a religious freak.

Not necessarily, Art. Not necessarily. That's why you're so damned lucky.

Me? I don't go to church.

You have your wife, Adeleine, and your beautiful daughter. I don't know how you do it, big guy, but I admire your abilities. You're a lucky son of a bitch, to have found decent female company. And God, on top of that, if your wife ever left you, I'm sure you'd be able to find another one just like that. Women just seem to like you.

Thanks.

You're lucky, Art. You are.

You're telling me?

How are you and Adeleine doing anyways?

Me and Adeleine? We have our problems. Don't get me wrong. It's not all roses. And Meg's a handful. At least for her dad...

But it's something, Art, right? At least you have people to go home to at the end of the day. You have people to think about. That's a good thing.

Yes, I suppose it is.

I'm happy for you, Art. I really am.

Cheers. To you.

No, to you, Art. You're my inspiration. God bless.

When I returned to the office I dropped my new gun and the rounds of ammo on the shelf next to the champagne glasses. Where else was I going to put it? In the safe? Maybe the safe was the right answer, but I was too tired or lazy to fuck with the combo. And maybe Cal was right, maybe you needed to be able to get to a gun quickly or it was no good.

After that I went home to bed and just forgot about it.

⊙

I stand over my wife's grave and I can't believe she's dead.

She has been dead five years, and after five years the difficulty of believing she is dead has not gone away.

People always telling me to forget it. Get it behind you. What's done is done. The past is dead. Move forward. But I always say, it's so easy telling somebody to forget. Telling someone is easy as pie. All you have to do is say it, and you move on unscathed. But for me, I wasn't unscathed by the incident. It really broke me. I mean snapped me in two. Broken. Broken. Busted. Just cracked in half. Unfixable. I didn't think at first I would be so broken by this. But time doesn't seem to have made it any easier. I kept figuring time was going to be my friend on this, but time has failed me. Let time heal you, as they say. But time hasn't healed a thing. Only made things worse. None of my wounds are healed. If anything, it's only gotten more painful with time.

I have a hard time sleeping. I can't concentrate. If I lacked motivation to get out of bed before she was killed, it's been impossible now. It's the reason why I always show up late to work. I show up and there's Wanda looking all bright and fresh as springtime flowers and I'm always half dead because I couldn't sleep because all that was going through my head during the night was how she was killed. So much for counting sheep...and for what?

There were over eighty people from all walks of life at her funeral. Six people stood up to eulogize her. I was asked if I wanted to say a few words. But what could I say? That the whole thing was a desecration? Just a fucking desecration, and that I was to blame? Stop blaming yourself, people tell me. That's bullshit. Take responsibility for your actions is what I say. I was the reason—me and no one else is why this whole tragic thing happened. Had I been more responsible with the Glock, none of this would have happened. Had I decided upon a different career—as she had suggested— none of this would have happened. But my wife was very supportive of me. She was supportive of Meg as well. She always told both of us, whatever we want to be we can be. She said she'd support us 110%. What was I to say about her at her funeral? That she was behind me 110%? That I was too stubborn to change my ways? That the reason why I was in this business in the first place was because it was a lark?

At the funeral, those who did get up to talk spoke about what an angel she was. And the truth is, my wife was an angel. How else to describe her, but to say she was as sweet as can be? She worked like hell, and I understand she could be tough at work, but she was one of those rare birds who also had a gentle sweetness to her. There is no getting around that. You could see it not only in the way she and Meg got along, but with everyone else as well. She was a very unique individual. Everyone loved her. I still don't know why she hooked up with me, of all people. She could have gotten anyone she wanted.

I remember the first time I met her parents. I could see it in their eyes even then—they wondered where in the hell their daughter had found such a creature. They thought our relationship was a temporary thing. Back then, even I thought it was temporary. But of course it wasn't. We actually loved each other. It was good chemistry. Adeleine and I fit well together: her hand in my hand, her body against my body. It was as if we had been designed to physically complete each other. As I got older my body changed, and so did hers, but that fitting one body against the next didn't change. We grew together through the years, and we always seemed to fit. We were one of those couples, the older we got the more we resembled each other. Our attitudes about life were also complimentary. I'm plodding. Unflappable. Set in my ways. She always said I was like a well-built house. Straight walls built upon a strong foundation. Adeleine had similar qualities of perseverance. But she was more graceful than I was. She was flexible, where I was fixed. It was this that really gave me a lot of security. When I saw that flexibility in her, it made me feel she understood me and that she could handle who I was.

Before I met Adeleine, no one seemed to understand me. My mother and father didn't understand me. My father always felt I fell short of my potential. I never knew what my potential was—that is the problem. What's more, there was so much out there that people seemed to want, and the thing about me is, I never wanted it. It seems to me that rising to the occasion of one's potential is partly related to wanting, so on some level my problem was, and is, I don't want enough. I want just enough to get along, that's all. Nothing more. As to money, I don't give a damn about it. Everybody obsessed with money—as if it can make you happy! Certainly the lack of money may make you unhappy, but it's never been proven that an excess of money will make you more happy.

What's important is that you figure out how to be happy with who you are—and this was a view that Adeleine and I both shared. But my dad didn't understand my type of happiness. He was an immigrant from Poland, and he didn't understand how I could be happy not wanting anything at all. He also sensed I was prone to laziness. All he understood was hard work. If you have time on your hands, he liked to tell me...

If you have time on your hands, Art...

Yes Dad.

It seems you have too much time on your hands.

What do you mean?

What I mean is, if you have too much time on your hands, maybe you're not working hard enough. Maybe you ought to consider working a little harder than you appear to be working.

For what reason, Dad? I'm happy.

Bah. Happy! You need to be successful.

How successful? Successful like you?

Well I certainly want you to be more successful than me.

But you're successful enough, Dad. Look at you. You have Mom and me. There's Jason. You have a nice house in the suburbs. A good job...

But you with your brains, Art. You can do more than me. You should go farther. The son should always improve on the father. The father lays the foundation; the son builds the building. That's the way it is from one generation to the next.

But I don't want your life. I'm happy with the life I have.

But the life you have, don't forget, is provided to you free of charge from me. And don't think I'm going to bankroll you forever.

I didn't realize that's how you thought of it, Dad— that you were bankrolling me.

When you're a child, Art, you're a child. You can be whatever you want to be. But when you're a man, you'll have to learn how to stand on your own.

I don't know if I wanted to stand on my own. I wanted human connection, and I found that with Adeleine.

I remember when I met Adeleine, one of the first things she told me was she could tell I was happy. She really admired that in me. I admired it in her, too. And it was then, I suppose, when a bond began to form. We even talked about it.

There is something here, isn't there, Adeleine?

What do you mean?

A bond. Do you feel a bond forming between us?

And in mock silliness she would say back to me, countering my seriousness:

Yes, I see a bond forming between us, Art. It is a strong bond. It is a bond meant to last. It is a bond that is unbreakable and we will stay cemented to each other forever and ever until death do us part.

At which point she would begin laughing, and I would begin laughing, and at such times the death-do-us-part bit seemed like it would never happen. Not to us. Things like death-do-us-part happen to others. But it spares happy people such as ourselves.

Of course, it didn't end up sparing us. It got us just like it got everyone else. Sooner or later the seeds of our own destruction are planted, and sometimes they grow before we are ready. Or as she once so unforgettably said, remember the monstrosity you evoke may come home to sleep with you.

Such was the case with my Adeleine, and with my determination to stick with the detective business.

⊙

My wife wasn't in the ground two weeks when I got a call from the bricklayer.

Let's meet, he said.

OK?

We need to talk.

Where would you like to meet?

How about that coffee shop?

It was a hot day. The sun was beating down. I waited in a courtyard outside the coffee shop. There were a few tables in the courtyard and a fountain that was spraying water. The courtyard was empty but I had a good view of the place so it seemed strategically the best place to meet him. It was a safe public place. Nothing would ever happen here. But then again, maybe anything in the world could happen anywhere. Adeleine's death had taught me that much. I felt sick to my stomach, but I sat there waiting for him. Since Adeleine died, I had no taste for strangers. I also had a funny feeling about this meeting, so I'd brought my Ruger. I'd loaded it with live rounds and holstered it in a Bianchi leather waistband holster that Cal, in a fit of generosity, had given me. I did not feel righteous.

I wished for alcohol instead of coffee, but coffee it was. I stared up at the sky half worrying some malign act was going to fall down upon me, and half hoping to see her up there smiling down on me.

Hi, Art.

Hi, Adeleine.

How are you?

Terrible. Devastated. Crushed. Broken. I could go on, but I won't. I want to hang myself from a rope in the garage and call it quits. Suicide is the only true medicine in cases like this. I don't have the heart to shoot myself. Not after what happened to you. I'm sorry what happened to you. I truly am.

I'm sorry too, Art. It's not what we discussed, is it?

No, Adeleine. This is not what we planned. Suddenly the appetite for life has escaped me. I've stopped eating. I go days on end like this, and then suddenly I realize I'm on the cusp of starvation so I binge-eat to catch up. My heart races at night and I wish it would just blow so I could be done with it, but the heart is a strong organ. I wish you were here with me.

You're on your own now.

Meg left me.

I'm sorry.

I want her to return. We love her so very much, don't we honey?

Yes we do.

Then there he was all of a sudden. The bricklayer.

•

He came loping from around the corner. By the looks of him I was glad I had my gun. He shouted: Hello detective. He insisted I stand up so he could shake my hand. His hands trembled.

I didn't budge.

Get up, detective. Stand up! I want to shake your hand.

I got up and reached my hand out. I thought to punch the shit out of him and crack his skull open, but I was wary. He grabbed my hand with both hands, and brutally squeezed it; he shook it up and down like a water pump.

Hello, detective, he said. Good to see you again, he says. Thanks for coming out today! Jesus it's hot. Are you drinking coffee, detective? Good, I'm glad you're drinking coffee. That's what detectives like you do for a living, apparently. You sit in coffee shops drinking coffee while the rest of us work. You sit in coffee shops like vultures waiting to feast on your next meal.

Listen, it was you who called me to come out today.

Yessir. Sit, detective. Please. Sit down. Please. I'm glad you came. Now sit down. Relax. I want you to sit and be calm, detective. This is between friends, because I want to ask you something.

Shoot.

No, sit first. Please sit, detective.

So I sat. I looked at my watch and I informed him I wasn't getting paid for this.

No need for payment here. This is just a friendly visit, but I want to ask you a question. A serious question. You asked me some questions, a few weeks ago. Now do you mind if I ask you a question or two, detective?

I remained silent.

OK then. Let me speak and I will ask it. Suppose someone, detective. Suppose some person tried to take your wife away from you.

Yes.

Let me ask you that again, detective. Suppose there were some person who tried to take your wife away from you...

Yes. I heard the question. What's your point?

My point is this. If someone tried to legally or physically take your wife away from you...

Listen, I said, interrupting him. I don't know what this is about. But I'm not trying to take your wife or anybody else's wife away from them. I'm off your case. I signed off on your case. I don't want your case. Frankly, I don't need the business. What's happening to you is between you and your wife. If your wife is leaving you or asking you to leave her then I recommend you take it up with her. Or get your own lawyer to defend you. But frankly, there's no reason for us to be having this discussion right now. I wish you well. I also wash my hands of all this. Now if you don't mind, this conversation is over.

But detective. The thing you don't understand is...

The thing I don't understand? Are you trying to tell me I don't understand? Because if you are, I'm going to ask you to lay off. There's plenty in this world I don't understand. That being said I don't need you to clarify anything for me.

But the thing you don't understand, detective, and the reason why I asked you to come out today is because I want to know something, and you're not answering me.

I'm leaving. I'm leaving now.

But supposing, detective. Supposing someone out of the blue tried to take your wife away from you, whether by law or by force. How would you feel about that?

Someone did take my wife.

How would you feel if you knew who it was?

Supposing you shut your mouth.

Supposing, detective, you answer me. That's why we're here today. That's why we're meeting like this. It's just a simple conversation between friends. How would you feel?

•

Art, promise me one thing.

Yes, Adeleine, anything...

Promise me one thing, is all.

I promise, honey.

Promise me that if I should die before you to bury me in a pine box...

•

Detective. Do you hear me? Are you listening to me? Suppose...

What the hell is all this about?

It was I, detective, who shot your wife.

I'm listening.

This is the gun that killed your wife.

He pulled a gun from his pocket and set it on the table. It was the Glock 26 with the rubberized grip that Cal had given me. I was speechless.

So he went on: You didn't know it was gone, did you? You didn't even know it was gone from your closet.

Again I couldn't talk.

I'm sorry, detective, for killing your wife, but I did it. I killed her. And we can't go back to fix what has been done, can we? I don't know what got into me, detective. You got into me, I suppose. You sitting there in your coffee shop trying to steal my wife away from me. I didn't like your attitude while you sat and asked me those questions and I didn't like that you recorded me on that recorder of yours without asking me. I didn't like that you recorded my story without even thinking of asking me if it was OK to record my story. And then later, after we had our little conversation, it occurred to me that I had nothing but a litigious wife, who herself had a lawyer who wanted to do me in, and now a detective who had recorded evidence of our conversation. I couldn't stand that you stole my voice away from me, detective, on that little recorder of yours, and that once you stole my voice, my voice would be used to steal my wife away from me. What's more, you got into me so I didn't feel like myself anymore.

I just sat there and took it all in. I did not know what I was supposed to say to any of this. So he went on.

So I wanted to take out my anger on you, detective. I found out where you work. I looked up your AAAgency. I didn't know what I was doing. I went up the elevator of your building in the early evening, and when I got off the elevator I saw the door to your office was open. Your door wasn't even locked! I turned the knob. It opened, so I stepped inside. No one was in it. Your office was immaculately clean. I didn't know what I was doing, exactly, or why I was in your office, but once I got in there I did have an idea to try and find that recording you made of me. I was pissed off like hell at you and that dirty lawyer of hers. I wanted to show you what it means to lose something. You have a nice office, detective. Your business must pay well for such a nice office on Jewelers Row on Wabash Avenue. And what do you do with such a business? Go to coffee shops and try to steal wives away from men who work all day in the hot sun. I sat in your office chair and I tried to imagine what it must be like to be a detective who does such things. I saw the picture of your wife and daughter framed on your desk. I saw you had an office mate who probably took care of your office. I kicked my feet up on your desk, and the phone rang. When I picked it up, someone on the other end was asking for a plumber. I tried not to laugh. Is this how you make money, waiting to intercept people who are looking for someone who does honest work? Tricking them into inquiring about your services? I still didn't know what I was doing. But I was a detective. I was you, detective! I said in the calmest voice possible: No, this is the detective agency. Is there something I can do for you? When I said that the phone went dead. I was wearing my dirty work clothes caked in mortar. I wondered what it would be like to work in an air-conditioned office and not have to soil my clothes with mortar. I wondered what it would be like to sit in an air-conditioned office for a living. I noticed there was a small closet in your office with some of your clothes stored there and a shelf where you kept champagne and some glassware. I also saw a gun case, and I opened up, and there it was, your Glock. What the hell? I thought. I put it on the desk and put the case back. I took my clothes off and tried yours on. They looked like a fit. I didn't have to be a bricklayer. I could be a detective. I could be you! I put on your socks. I found a pair of pants and tried them on. They fit perfectly. I pulled out a flannel shirt, from Farm and Fleet, I think. It was one of the same exact shirts I own, detective. I was surprised to see all the work clothes in your closet! What is it you do that merits a workingman's clothes? As far as I can tell, detectives like you don't work for a living. Of course I took your Glock. It was there for the taking. It was loaded. And you didn't even know it was gone! What kind of detective are you, if you can't even detect a crime has taken place? But I wanted to be you. I wanted to be more you than you. I combed my hair with a comb you had in your desk drawer—did you notice I took that with me as well? Or did that escape your notice? How many things do you think escape your notice every single day? You go about your business so blithely, but what is it you really notice about your life? What do you really see, detective?

Again I just did not know what to say. So again he continued.

Then I walked around your office, detective. I walked around trying to figure out where you might have stored that recording. Then I found your safe and I was in the process of trying to break it open when I heard the elevator ping. I looked up and I saw a woman come off the elevator and toward your office. My first glimpse of her, I thought: How pretty! Who knows, there might have been a moment when she thought that I was you.

And she spoke. She said: Hello? Art? That's what she said. I won't forget your wife's voice, detective. She had a lovely voice. It was resonant, but contained octaves. With those words alone you could sense there was something sweet about her. That's how my wife used to sound, detective, when I came home from work. That was before she got messed up with that lawyer of hers. Before you involved yourself in the mess.

I took a deep breath like I was about to say something, but there were still no words. There were still no words. So he went on.

Your wife stepped through your office door, detective, and she saw me kneeling by your safe, and she didn't think twice about what she saw. She thought she saw you. In that moment I became, perfectly, you. I received her as you received her every day of your life together. When she asked how I was doing, I told her: Fine. Upon hearing my voice, she paused. I could sense her tense up and when she realized that I might not be you she backed out of your office and into the elevator foyer. At that moment, I was no longer you. The illusion was broken. And your Glock was right there. I picked it up and I shot her. *Pop. Pop. Pop. Pop. Pop.* I don't know what got into me, detective. I've never shot a thing in my life. I never intended to shoot anything. But the gun was right there and I couldn't stop. It just felt like the most natural thing in the world. Like the gun just appeared in my hand. Like it shot itself. It's a Glock. What can I say? I unloaded all seventeen rounds into her. She was lovely, really, in that black dress. It wasn't my plan to kill her, but then it was. I wanted to make you feel what you seemed unable to understand. I wanted you to feel my pain, detective. My final shot was right at her face. Between her eyes to put her out of her misery. I will tell you that before the final bullet was shot, she suffered. After I shot her, I wanted to kill myself, but there were no more bullets. So I walked home. It was a long walk, so it wore me out. When I got home I took a nap because I was tired.

Again I didn't know if it was my turn to talk, or if I could gain anything by talking.

Now my wife wants me back, detective. My wife wants me back. And she said so, only yesterday. So I wish I could return yours to you, but I can't do that. And that's why I'm here...to figure out what to do next.

I looked at the Glock 26 sitting on the table between us. It had a clip in it but I didn't know if the clip was loaded or not.

Go ahead, detective, he said. If that's what you want. Go ahead. Just shoot me. I'm OK with it.

I shifted in my chair, and maybe he thought I was making a move for the gun, but he didn't do anything. I backed off.

No, please. Be my guest, detective. Pick up the gun and shoot me.

She was a wonderful woman, I told him.

I imagine so, detective. I heard it in her voice.

No. You can't imagine.

OK, detective. Maybe I can't. Tell me...

She was wonderful beyond what you can imagine.

Then I'm sorry for your loss, detective...

There's no way for you to understand what you have done to me.

My wife tried to divorce me. I can understand a little of what it means to lose that.

That's not the same. It's not equal. This is worse. Much worse. I was only doing my job. I only asked you a few questions.

I'm sorry, detective. I never intended this. But I was possessed by you. And then of course, she walked through your office door. Can you believe that?

I can't believe I'm talking to you. I should kill you.

You still can, detective. There's your Glock. Go ahead and shoot. Put me out of my misery.

I'm not going to kill you. I'm going to call the police.

I called 911. I said: There's a potential killer with a loaded gun sitting at a table outside the cafe.

After I called the police I looked at him.

Can I buy you a coffee or something? he asked. While we wait for the police, detective?

No. I can't drink coffee right now.

I'm thirsty.

He reached for his glass of water, took a sip, and set his glass down.

I could hear the sirens in the distance. That's what I remember, though it makes no sense. Maybe those sirens belonged to a different crime or injury.

Why did you shoot her so many times? I asked.

Do you want to know the truth, detective?

Yes.

Because she reminded me of my wife. My wife, who also wanted to destroy me. I also wanted to send a message. I wanted to let you and her and everyone else to know that it's not OK to ruin a man's life like you ruined me.

I didn't ruin you. I was only doing my job. I have a daughter, you know. I had a family. I was put on earth to live in the circle of my family, happily. You took that all away.

It was a mistake, detective. Do you know, after the divorce proceedings, my wife asked to take me back! That's when I knew—you and me—we had to talk. My wife said she didn't like living alone without me. She couldn't handle the kids alone. She apologized for putting me through this turmoil. She said she didn't know what had gotten into her. She blamed it all on menopause. I don't deserve her.

I don't know why you're telling me this. I think you should tell the cops.

I wanted you to just shoot me. But instead, you called the police. Like a coward! Are you sure that was the right thing to do? That gun...your wife was killed with it. They'll see it was your gun. They'll figure that out, in their investigation.

He stared at me and smiled.

You're a detective. I can see you have a gun on you, too. Why don't you use it? What's the point, if you don't use it? Instead, you just sit there like a fucking coward! What kind of man are you, detective, that doesn't take his revenge? You could shoot me, but you don't! You call the police instead! Sure, let them do your dirty work! Fine. Here, I'll do it for you.

He moved swiftly and grabbed the Glock. He pointed it directly at me. I didn't flinch.

Go ahead, just shoot me.

He turned the gun on himself and put the barrel in his mouth. Then he pointed up towards the back of his head and fired. *POP.*

There was a flash of red. His body flopped forward on top of the table. There was a thud as if a heavy weight had fallen and then his arm dropped. The gun escaped his hand and hit the cement with a clatter. There was his eye staring straight at me just below the hole in his head that was suddenly leaking blood. I looked at that eye, and it saw me until it stopped seeing me.

I expected people to come running, but they didn't.

As I waited, my mouth grew dry. I reached for his glass of water; it hadn't toppled over, and I drank it. I set the empty glass on the table and looked up in the trees. A little bit of light was reflecting off the bark. That's what I noticed how even black bark could reflect light if the angle was just right. I saw the dark branches filled with sparrows. They had been startled by the gunshot from the pavement to the safety of the trees. In the shade underneath the awning of the coffee shop were a handful of pigeons pecking around at a crust of bread. One of the sparrows left its branch in the tree and flew to where the pigeons were in the shade of the awning. I expected people to come out of the coffee shop because of the gunshot, but no one seemed to notice what just happened. Only the sparrows seemed to notice. Another sparrow followed back to the pavement, and then another, and after a moment all the sparrows had flown to where the pigeons were, and there was a tussle for a few pieces of crust that were too big for any of the birds to fly away with. The bread looked to be the crust of a baguette. I preferred Wonder Bread for the birds because it had a softer, more malleable crumb. Nevertheless the pigeons and the sparrows would figure out how to break the crust, and if they couldn't break it apart one of the squirrels emerging from the garbage can would figure out how to break it apart and then the pigeons and sparrows would figure out how to rob the squirrel and get their morsel of bread anyway.

I watched the birds carefully. I don't care what anyone says of pigeons or sparrows or crows or grackles. I see a friend in these birds.

Then I looked up into the higher blue of the sky and all I saw were shadows circling around.

•

When the police came, they asked me to step aside. "Get outside the perimeter." One of the police actually pushed me so I almost stumbled backwards. "Step outside the perimeter." He was wearing blue surgical gloves. Another officer showed up by ATV vehicle. He wore a white motorcycle helmet. His radio receiver was firmly attached to a strap on his torso, and he spoke into it: Victim. Male. 48-55 years. Gunshot through mouth to top of head.

Then he turned to me and said:

Who was the dead body?

I told him it was the man who had killed my wife.

I pointed to the gun and I told him that I thought that was the gun he used to kill her. It was also the gun he used to kill himself. The Glock 26. Another officer snapped a picture of where the gun lay, then gathered it in a bag for evidence.

Did you know the dead body?

No.

Did you touch or disturb the dead body when the dead body fell?

No.

Did anyone touch or disturb the dead body when the dead body fell?

No.

As far as you know, did anyone else touch or observe the dead body when the dead body fell?

No.

Was the dead body dead when the dead body fell?

Yes.

And on the questions went. There was a pause and we went to the police station and then they asked the same questions again. And when they had taken down all the information they needed, I was released. Then nightfall came and I found myself out of doors and alone and wandering in the night.

⊙

Adeleine, I still don't know why you came by my office that night.

I came to see you, Art. I came to surprise you. I wore my favorite dress, the black one that you like. I thought we might go out to eat. I thought for once you and I would spend a Tuesday night downtown by ourselves at any restaurant you wanted to go to.

Or she might have said: I came to find out what you do all day. I still don't know what it is you do all day, because I can see by the money that you bring home that clearly you are not doing enough to cover your costs. When are you going to give up on this detective business and try something that rises to the occasion of your talent?

That was the exact word she might have used. Talent. Your talent, Art! You have so much talent to give. When are you going to let go of this business for which you were not made, and finally express the God-given talent you were born with?

Or she might have said: I've heard so much about Wanda, I stopped by to check on you. I have no idea what it is the two of you do all day locked up in this office that I pay for, but she does seem too pretty by half.

Or she might have said: Art, I love you more than words can say.

I love you too, honey, thanks for visiting. Only I'm sorry what happened.

Yes. I'm sorry too. I'm so sorry.

•

I want to forget having to tell my daughter that her mother's killer had been found.

The look on her face when she asked: Is he alive?

No.

How did he die?

He killed himself. He shot himself with his gun.

Do they know why he killed mom?

He only said that she got scared and he didn't know how to control her so he shot her. He also said he wanted me to understand...

Understand what?

Understand *his* pain...

He didn't have to shoot mom, dad. No one needed to shoot mom. Did you know the man? Was he related to your business?

I knew the man. I had interviewed him for a routine divorce case and something about that interview made him snap. I am so sorry, honey. I am so sorry that this happened.

She was crying now and charged me and she pushed me away.

This is all your fault, Dad.

She started pounding on my chest and shrieked at me in grief. Then she pushed me away again and coiled in a corner as far from me as she could get, sobbing.

Leave me alone, Dad. As long as I live I ask only that you leave me alone. That is the only forgiveness that you're ever going to get from me.

I sincerely want to forget the sound of the door slamming as she left me alone in the room.

The sound of the door, *bang*. And she was gone.

She moved in with her friend to finish senior year, and then she went to Tulane, and I never heard from her or saw her again, though on each anniversary of her mother's death I call and leave a message, hoping she'll pick up.

•

Cal steps back into the lane with his Uzi and lets it rip on full auto, shredding the paper target until it dances and then falls off the clips. It's a joy to watch him handle such a gun. His body vibrates to the action. The whites of his eyes are not so white. He keeps shooting a moment after the target falls. Little dark crescents form in the fold of flesh just beneath his eyes. He takes a breath, steps back and reloads.

I ask him: Cal...

Yes, my friend...

When are you going to pretend that I'm the target?

Say again?

He sticks a magazine clip like a shiv into the bottom of the gun and loads a round into the chamber.

When are you going to pretend that I'm the target? Just shoot me. Take me out of my misery.

He laughs.

Take me out of my misery. Like Tony Spilotro in that Indiana cornfield.

Like who?

Like Tony Spilotro.

He laughs again.

You laugh again.

You joke again.

I don't joke. Why don't we find a place? You pretend I'm the target. You could take me out. It would be painless. Drop me where I stand. Do it clean.

What's gotten into you, Art?

Nothing's gotten into me. Please. I want done with it. I'll even help dig the hole.

I don't have a shovel.

I'll buy you a goddamned shovel.

Not me, Cal says.

A friend would do this for me, Cal. Please. We'll find a place out in a remote field. I will stand as steady as you need me to stand, then you can unload on me. No hard feelings. You're the only one I can count on to put me out of my misery.

Art...

He shakes his head and steps back into the lane and he starts shooting semi auto, taking careful aim at the target, hunched over. *BLURT! BLURT! BLURT!* There's a mean and sleepless look in his eyes.

Cal, you need sleep, I shout.

You're telling me! He fires away in rapid succession: *BLUUURT! BLUUURT! BLUUUUURT!* I haven't slept in two nights!

I haven't either.

What's keeping you up, Art?

He switches back to full auto and leans forward. Then he squeezes the trigger, bullets flying all over the place. *BLUUUUUUUUUUURT!* It's a deadly weapon until it isn't. Then it's just a toy, and he loves shooting his toy at the paper target.

Seriously, he says, shooting and shouting at the same time. What keeps you up at night, Art?

I need you to understand me, Cal. My wife has been dead for five years and I gave it the scout's try. Honest!

It's time to move on, buddy. *BLUUUURT!*

OK. I'm moving on.

BLURT BLUT BLURT. Asshole, he says under his breath, then he starts again with the Uzi. He shoots for another ten or fifteen seconds until there's nothing left of the target and when he's done he lowers his gun and pauses a moment trying to regain the reality of not shooting a machine gun. His eyes are still vibrating. After he adjusts, he smiles.

Then he says, hold on, Art, I wanna give you something. He leaves the gun range for a second and goes back to his car. When he returns he has a gun in a holster. It's a Glock 26. It looks familiar.

Take a break from your pussy gun, Arthur, and try this on for size.

Haven't we had this conversation already?

We have.

Then why are we having it again?

It's a cure. Hair of the dog that bit you, Art. Why don't you give it a try?

I stare at it again. Is it the same gun? It looks like the same gun. Can it be the same gun? The cops had taken it and put it in evidence. I'd never told them I'd had it. It seemed like it would be more trouble than it was worth to sort it all out, with me having been under investigation and all. But there was a serial number. Had they called the gun show people? Had they tracked down Cal? What had they told him? What had he told them—that it was stolen? I stare at it again...

I'm tired of seeing you shoot that Ruger. Why not give it a try? It's only a gun. And a nice one at that.

He holds it in his outstretched hands for me to take.

I can't do it, Cal. Sorry.

Go on. Give it a try. Think of it as medicine. I promise it will help.

Adeleine.

She's gone, Art. Let her go. It's time for you to live on your own two legs. Besides, just so you know...because you're a friend, I customized it for you. For instance, I put on this Pearce extension grip for those big hands of yours. I also put tritium sights on, which was a bitch, but it'll be great at low light levels. It's got the seventeen-round magazine clip too. Go ahead, give it a try. I want you to have it, to honor all the years of our friendship. Really, there's no reason not to. Give it a try. You'll see. No need to be a big baby about it. Besides, I remember how you loved this gun. How well you shot with it.

He makes a little bow and holds the gun out in both hands and waits for me.

OK, Cal. If you put it that way, what am I gonna do?

The way Cal outfitted it, the gun fits nice in my hand. I push a small button and out comes the fully loaded seventeen-round magazine clip, quick and easy. I check the chamber to make sure there isn't a round in it. Then I put the clip back in the gun and sight at a target. I like the sights considerably more. They really jump out now. I holster the gun. I stand there a moment looking at what I'm going to shoot. I take a breath. I draw the gun and sight at the target. I try to separate from my emotions, and then I start firing.

You like it, big guy? Cal says.

Perfect for an old man. Thank you, I reply.

It's about time you hit the target again.

I unload another clip while Cal stands there goading.

How does it feel? Cal says.

Alive again. I haven't felt this great in years. Thank you for the gun, Cal. It's easy on the bones.

Yeah, and your accuracy is great. Better than ever.

It's the tritium sight. It is really nice.

He hands me the clip. I load, drop a round in the chamber, and start firing. It is still amazing how the gun shoots compared to my old Ruger. Also, the stippled grip that Cal outfitted it with helps it sit firmly in my hand despite the fast shooting action.

Don't you see? It's a better gun for you than that Ruger.

Yes, I say, banging away at the target.

Look at you go, big guy! I ain't never seen anything like it. Your accuracy is through the roof! I'm loving what I'm seeing here. You might be a sniper after all!

I might be!

I drop another magazine and then another magazine. I want right then and there to give the Glock the name of my first-born child—the child I had before I had the child that I had: I want to call the gun Luke.

Just think about that fuck Adolph Meyer, Cal says. Think about that fuck, and what he did to you.

And suddenly I saw my wife. And once I saw my wife, I couldn't unsee her. All the wounds. And then Adolph Meyer. That puff of red.

I've had enough.

I put the Glock in its case and thank Cal.

I'm done, I say. I'm done shooting this gun.

I bend down, pick up a spent 9 mm casing, blow on it, then put it in my pocket as a souvenir.

Thank you very much, Cal, I say, for the experience of shooting this gun. I've learned something, and now I'm done.

Didn't you like it?

Yes.

Don't you want to keep it?

No, you hold on to it.

You sure? You did well with it. I'm super proud of what you showed me here.

And what's that?

That you know how to shoot.

OK. Now it's your turn. Go ahead and shoot, Cal.

He steps up to the lane with his Uzi and casts a glance at me like he's trying to tell me something. Then he goes apeshit with the machine gun, tearing up the target sideways and backwards. It's a marvel to watch the man shoot. I know what he's shooting at, too. When he's through, he swears.

God! Jesus! Holy shit that was fun, he says, setting down the Uzi so it can cool off. I feel a helluva lot better! How about you, Art?

I still want to buy a shovel.

But Cal isn't even listening: Outstanding, my friend! Outstanding. Nothing like shooting to fix what's wrong with you. It liberates the soul. How about let's do it again soon?

How about it? Only next time in a cornfield.

Now I'm watching Albert Volares' mom deal with the grief. It helps me forget my own grief. I thought I suffered. And here she is about to explode—a whole journey of suffering awaiting her. Another feast after the feast that followed the funeral. A bitter feast to be eaten alone in the dark of night while everyone else sleeps.

A woman who looks like she could be Rita's sister steps up to the mound of dirt and shovels a clod onto Albert's casket. She sets the spade down and steps aside, sobbing. Who was this Albert Volares? Fifteen years old...and dead. He probably didn't know what hit him. That's the hope at least: that he lost consciousness mercifully quick. But in all likelihood, he probably didn't. He probably suffered a great deal for what he was about to lose: the whole rest of his life. What was I doing when I was fifteen? What did I do to earn the whole rest of my life?

•

A kid standing next to me is wearing a football jersey.

He was paralyzed from the neck down, the kid says.

Oh…

I visited him in the hospital.

You did?

He was my best friend.

I'm sorry.

He wanted to be an FBI agent.

Yes, I see.

He fell into a coma soon after he was carried off of the football field. He played running back.

I'm sorry, I tell the kid.

He never woke up.

How long did he survive after he died?

Three weeks. He had tubes in and out of his nose and mouth. It was terrible.

The priest signals for a moment of silence.

The shoveling pauses, and then it continues. The thudding of dirt on the casket.

•

After Albert Volares' funeral, the father hands out cards and directions to the restaurant. He hands one out to all of the relatives. I watch him hand cards to some of the kids who came over on the bus. The kid in the football jersey waves his hand at it, declining to accept.

You sure? The dad seems perplexed. You're welcome to come.

No. Sorry, sir. I have to take the school bus back. I have weight training.

Weren't you friends with Albert?

The boy shakes his head yes. Yes, sir. Yes I was, as a matter of fact.

I would love for you to come to dinner with us. Why don't you come? We can talk about Albert. I'll see that you get home afterwards.

The boy looks at his friends. They shrug their shoulders. Unable to stand up to the man's grief and curiosity, the boy assents. Fine, I'll come.

You can drive along in the limo with us. There's plenty of room.

He walks over to the three youths.

And how about you guys. Would you like to join us?

No thank you, sir, says the boy with the pink housecoat. His face is aflame with pimples, his hair blows wild in the wind, as does his pink housecoat.

Please. Join us. I insist. There will be pasta, pizza...all sorts of things to eat.

No thanks, sir. The boy looks at the father unblinkingly, looks him straight in the eyes, and the man stares back at the boy. They stand there looking into each other's eyes. Thinking and seeing who knows what.

Please, I insist. The father puts his hand on the boy's shoulder.

I didn't know him.

The father looks slightly surprised, but nonplussed. Please, why don't you and your friends join us anyway? You were here for our grief; the least you can do is let me feed you. A skinny guy like you, you must be hungry.

OK, the boy says. Alright sir, but we would need a ride.

Please, we have plenty of room in the limos.

The father walks over to me.

Hi, he says, handing me a card to the restaurant. Thank you for coming. Were you one of Albert's teachers?

For a moment I don't know what to say. I feel caught in an act of voyeurism. I have been standing at the periphery of the funeral observing their grief—for what, I cannot begin to say—and now he's cornered me before I had the opportunity to get safely away. I smile sympathetically and shake my head no.

I'm sorry, I say. I never knew him.

Are you with them? He nods towards the kids.

No. I'm by myself.

What brings you here then?

The grave. His grave is located next to my wife's. It was to be my grave, but I hadn't gotten around to purchasing it yet from the cemetery. I came out today to visit her. It's the fifth anniversary of her burial. You'll have to forgive me; I didn't mean to intrude.

He looks taken aback again. He might be my contemporary, my exact age. By the looks of him, we may have even gone to high school together. Like these schoolmates here, we too may very well have been schoolmates once. Young once, just like these kids, our whole lives spread out ahead of us. Once...

I'm sorry, he says. I'm sorry about the grave. It's the one they assigned us. I didn't even think to ask.

It's alright. First come, first served. Unfortunately for your son and for you, he came first.

Yes, it is unfortunate.

It's terrible. I'm sorry.

He looks at me, then places a hand on my shoulder. I wish you could have known my son, he says. He was something else.

I believe it.

No. I mean that. He was something else. Every parent will tell you that their kid was something else if you give them half a chance—no surprise there. But my son, Albert, he *was* something else. I'm not stretching the truth on this.

Just then a small smile breaks out on his face. Oh, shucks. He was a good kid. He says it again: Oh, shucks. Such a waste...He had his whole life in front of him. Now he's gone. But he will be missed.

My very sincerest condolences, sir. Believe me. I know whereof you speak.

Do you?

Oh hell, I don't know. I just mean to say, if you're suffering: Believe me, I know suffering. Perhaps nothing like what you're going through. But if it's anything like what I've been going through—anyway, I do offer my sincerest condolences.

He looks me in the eye. I have the missus to look after. That helps. I'm too busy worrying about her at the moment to worry about myself. She's so hurt she wants to die.

I'm sorry.

Listen, why don't you join us anyway? It'll be nice to have you. No need hanging out in a graveyard. A little Italian place just down the road not far from here. You can practically walk there. Here's the address. You're welcome to join us. Maybe you'll learn something of my boy.

Thank you, I say, taking the card. But I'm not much for these affairs.

Whatever you decide.

•

The kid in the pink housecoat walks over to me.

I saw him talking to you.

Yes.

If you go, we'll go.

I don't have a car.

That's OK. The man said we could walk to the restaurant, didn't he?

I know the place, actually, I say. I've been there before. It's not far. Just outside the cemetery gate and past the intersection. I'll walk out with you.

Good, says the kid in the housecoat. I always wanted to ride in a limo, but I'll wait to do that. I don't want to ride one out of a graveyard. It seems like bad luck.

The other kids walk over.

What's the deal?

We're walking over, the kid in the pink housecoat says.

Walking? Shit!

It's not far, I say, trying to sound matter-of-fact, not cool.

Cool, the third kid says. If it's not far, then sure. Why not?

Did you know Albert? The girl asks as we walk down the winding road of the cemetery.

No.

You're not like, his teacher or something, are you?

No.

Or a coach or something? I heard he broke his neck in a football accident.

The autumn leaves shake loose in the cool wind.

Hey look, the girl says. That pond looks nice.

She strides off ahead and we follow. The four limos are filing out of the cemetery. A train of cars follows closely behind. At the end of the line is the school bus. When the last car turns right onto the road, the school bus turns left and heads in the opposite direction.

We stand near the pond looking at the calm surface of the water.

Serenity Pond. I love the name, don't you?

It's a funeral home name.

It's still a nice name. Serenity.

We stand at the edge of the water. Staring at it.

Why were you here today? the boy in the housecoat asks.

The girl turns to look at me, as does the other boy.

I came because of my wife. I'm here to pay respects to my wife. I came to visit her.

How did she die? You don't seem old enough to have a dead wife.

Shut up, the girl says. You can die young of breast cancer. Don't you know anything?

The boy in the housecoat suddenly looks as if he felt stupid.

I'm sorry, he says. I forgot about cancer.

How long ago did she die?

Five years ago. This is the fifth anniversary of her death.

And you're still coming to visit her grave?

Yes.

You must miss her.

More than words can say...

I'm sorry, the boy in the pink housecoat says.

No need for you to be sorry.

I am too, says the girl. You must have loved her very much.

I did. Yes.

I suppose you still love her, the other boy says.

The boy in the pink housecoat says: How can he love her? She's dead. The proper tense here is the past tense.

The girl says: Don't be so callous, Bert. Can't you see he must still love her? Love doesn't ever go in the past tense if it's true love.

The second boy laughs.

I suppose you're right, I tell her. That's a good observation.

But you're not loving the person, Bert says. Don't you see? You're loving the memory of the person.

The second boy says, Serenity Pond. Doesn't that say it all? There's all this chaos in our house...my father always screaming at my mother. We need a pond like this.

Yeah, Kim says. I like that idea. Serenity Pond. Smack dab in the center of Kevin's house.

All the kids laugh. Bert looks especially funny in his pink housecoat.

We start walking again up the drive that leads out of the cemetery.

When we come to the intersection outside of the cemetery, I point the restaurant out to the kids. See it over there?

Traffic passes by while we wait for the crosswalk light to turn. All these people, alone in their cars...

Hey, cool, thanks, says the kid in the pink housecoat. He confers with his friends a moment. The girl turns to me and says: Actually, sir. We have somewhere else to go instead.

See you, I say, and watch them go.

•

I stand a moment and wait.

That's when I decide to call my daughter. I miss her. I want her back in my life. I want a daughter again. I pull out my phone and ring her up. She picks up immediately.

Hello Meg.

Hi Dad.

She sounds drunk.

Are you drinking?

Why are you calling me?

I'm calling to say that this is her anniversary.

I know.

This is the fifth anniversary of mom's death.

I know, Dad! I have a fucking calendar.

I called to say hi.

Hello, Dad.

Hello, Meg.

Why don't you ever call me when it's not about Mom? Why do you only call this day? This fucking anniversary!

I can call any day you like.

Why haven't you, Dad?

I don't know.

I do.

Why's that, Meg?

Because you're a fucking coward!

I'm a coward?

You don't know how to move on, Dad! You don't know how to live life! You're stuck. You're tongue-tied. You were tongue-tied with Mom.

Mom and I had a perfect relationship.

Yeah. OK. If that's what you say, I suppose I'll believe it.

Meg...

Yes.

I'm sorry.

That's not enough.

I never meant to let you down and I let you down. I'm sorry for letting you down.

That's not enough either, Dad.

OK, fine. How about we start with a simple question...where are you?

I'm in Japan. Where the fuck do you think I am, Dad?

I have no idea. That's why I asked.

I'm in Tokyo eating sushi. And next stop I'm going to the moon. Where are you, Dad?

I don't know. I feel like I've been wandering in the wilderness and I want to stop wandering. I want to go home.

So do I. I want to go home to the place before any of this ever happened.

I want to be your father again.

I'm tired of all your bullshit lies.

I can tell you the truth. I can tell you that I'm an asshole. I can tell you that I'm lost. I've lost the roadmap and I'm wandering. I'm with a woman named Rita, and I've been with her almost as long as your mother has been dead. And she and I are not meant to be, and we were never meant to be. I can tell you that I would give anything to be your father again. I always liked how you dressed. Your mother and I were always so proud of you. I still am. Here's another true thing: I'm looking for serenity. I can't find it without you.

Well, here's what I can say, Dad: I'm drunk. I'm still living in New Orleans. I never finished Tulane. I've had two abortions and I drink too much. I suppose I love you. You have my number. Maybe next time you can figure out how to reach me on a different day of the year. My birthday, for fuck's sake! Maybe call me then. Dad, you really let me down. You would have disappointed Mom as well, in time. I'm not surprised her family doesn't talk to you. Everybody knows it was all your fault. And you were a freak at her funeral, and you never apologized for that, either.

I'm sorry. I apologize.

For what?

For everything.

You've got a long way to go before I accept. If I accept.

Please accept my apology.

I'll talk to you later. I gotta go. I can't talk any more right now. I need to vomit.

Goodbye, darling.

My daughter hangs up.

The traffic rushes by on the road. Everyone is going somewhere except for me. I'm just wandering. What the hell else am I to do? Tremble and vomit. What else is there to do?

•

From the ashes grows a flower, or so I thought.

Now you're rhyming again.

No, that's not true.

Yes it is!

I'm dying again.

Blurt. Blurt.

Pop. Pop. Pop.

•

There's winter in the air. It's far colder than it should be this time of year, and all of a sudden I'm frozen to the bone. When the light turns red, I look left and I look right. I pray there aren't any cars coming to knock me over. When I see all is clear I cross the street over to the restaurant where the limousines are parked and the folks inside are gathered around the feast for Albert. Then, hoping no one will see me, I pass by the restaurant and I just keep walking...

AUTHOR'S NOTE

June 29, 2017

Last night there was a steady rain, which was pleasant to hear in the late evening in the final waking minutes of my day. Water droplets were plinking on my window unit air conditioner, and occasionally through the window, flashes of lightning would burst from the darkness. Just as I was putting the final touches on this book (which has been, for me, a long meditation on the pain of gun violence), I heard several loud pops ring out in the alley not a few hundred yards away from my apartment. There were between a dozen and quite possibly seventeen pops. We are on the cusp of the Fourth of July holiday, so naturally I wanted to believe that what I heard was the opening rounds of firecrackers going off into the holiday weekend. But I had my doubts. Who sets off firecrackers in the rain? Who starts the firecracker jubilee on the 28th of June at 11:15 pm? Also, what firecrackers resound with such intentionality? They were loud bangs too, almost like M80s.

By the time I walked down the hallway to my bedroom, I heard the tell-tale sirens from several police vehicles and ambulances arrive on the scene telling me that what I had heard was a shooting, which suggested to me that I had witnessed the death of another victim brought down in the epidemic of gun violence that has shaken our city.

Or maybe it was just firecrackers. So far this morning, I haven't seen any trace of a neighborhood shooting in the news.

This gun violence, which is at the beating heart of our American identity, is something I wanted to address as a writer.

My own brother loved guns. He lived in a rural Illinois community at the far end of a gravel road that petered out into a dirt trail where stood his ramshackle dwelling—literally, from my vantage point, in the middle of nowhere. He was a hunter and he loved shooting animals not just for sport, but also for the hell of it. (Not unlike Zhmukhin's sons, so wonderfully described in Chekhov's story, *The Pecheneg*.) My brother also had set up several targets on his property and with plenty of artillery and ammunition he loved to have friends down to go plinking.

Later in his life he moved north to Fargo. He told me a story once. He said he asked a cop in Fargo if he could drive around North Dakota with a loaded gun in his truck. The cop told him that not only did he not care if my brother drove around North Dakota with a loaded gun in his truck, it was OK with him if he drove around with a loaded gun in his mouth.

Eventually, my brother, who had been kicked out of the economy (and whose social isolation contributed to his alcoholism, or vice versa) found himself out of money and out of luck in Pierre, South Dakota. He left his favorite watering hole and drove to his favorite fishing hole outside of town where there was nothing but open land in all directions, and he finally did as that cop suggested. He sat in his truck and he put a loaded gun in his mouth and he shot himself. He was a victim of that other epidemic of gun violence raging across America: suicide of white males over fifty years old.

The problem for me about writing about gun violence in the city is that other than hearing it through my window at night, and reading about it in the newspapers, it is mostly gang-related violence which has devolved into a chaotic Hatfield and McCoy grudge match of vengeance and counter vengeance. I have no connection to the gang violence here on the South Side of Chicago other than it happens in my neighborhood and community, and in that sense I am a victim of it. (Therefore, send not to know/For whom the bell tolls/It tolls for thee.) Yet as a novelist I can't write about this type of gang-related gun violence from a position of authority. I can, however, write a book about guys like my brother, and that's what I attempted to do with this book.

Harold Pinter's poem *Death* really shook me up when I first read it, and I used it as a guide to show me how to write about gun violence. I also wrote my own poem on the subject, which a previous shooting on a previous summer night in a previous alley had inspired me to write. I include it here.

TONIGHT IN THE STREETS

Tonight in the streets gunfire
and in the newspapers gunfire
and in the magazines gunfire
and on the TV screens gunfire
and in the alleyways of my imagination gunfire
and I lie on bed sheets frightened
though not obsessed
with this casual relationship we hold
to violence and not just violence
that kills mercifully—
gunstrike to heart or temple—
but to the violence that metes out daily
and incomprehensible life long
suffering to survivors like you or me:
the dark hole of violence that defying all odds
brushes up close and forces acknowledgment
of these strong ties' fragile knots.
And I'm frightened though not obsessed
with violence that
splits spine parapalegically
cripples hand and
teaches how to write
differently
wounds brain
dumbs tongue
blanks memory
not to mention kidney wounds
not to mention lung wounds

not to mention heart wounds
but I am not obsessed with this
though I can't escape the feeling
I'll encounter my fate
one summer afternoon
crows flocking the trees
drawing my attention
upward from the street
to the soft beat of their dark wings.

A NOTE OF THANKS:

I would like to thank everyone who has helped me along the way with this book. Shalini Prachand is a dear friend who reads all of my books before anyone else does and in so doing, gives me great encouragement. Bruce Franklin's friendship, enthusiasm, and daily conversation has helped continuously throughout the entire project. Ditto that for Saleem Dhamee. Sonny Garg helped with the title of the book. I had several important conversations on the topic of gun violence and how to represent it with the sculptor and artist Garland Martin Taylor, whose art is an inspiration to me. My sister, Cat, listened to me talk endlessly about this book and then she designed the brilliant cover that graces it. My editor and publisher, Jerry Brennan, is a great writer, and his passion made this book considerably better than the manuscript I had first sent to him. And for that, I thank him.

ABOUT THE AUTHOR

Joseph G. Peterson is the author of the novels *Beautiful Piece*, *Wanted: Elevator Man*, and *Gideon's Confession*. He has also written a book-length poem, *Inside the Whale*, and most recently a short-story collection, *Twilight of the Idiots*. He grew up in Wheeling, Illinois and now lives in Chicago where he works in publishing and lives with his family.

"One of my new favorite authors [is] Joseph G. Peterson." - Rick Kogan, WGN Radio

ABOUT TORTOISE BOOKS

Slow and steady wins in the end, even in the publishing industry. Tortoise Books is dedicated to finding and promoting quality authors who haven't yet found a niche in the marketplace—writers producing memorable and engaging works that will stand the test of time.

Learn more at www.tortoisebooks.com.

9 780998 632568